LINDA

April 4, 2006

Rude Promenade

BEST WISHES
& THANK YOU.

ENJOY.

by John Stephens

John Stephens

Bloomington, IN Milton Keynes, UK

authorHOUSE™

AuthorHouse™
1663 Liberty Drive, Suite 200
Bloomington, IN 47403
www.authorhouse.com
Phone: 1-800-839-8640

AuthorHouse™ UK Ltd.
500 Avebury Boulevard
Central Milton Keynes, MK9 2BE
www.authorhouse.co.uk
Phone: 08001974150

This book is a work of fiction. People, places, events, and situations are the product of the author's imagination. Any resemblance to actual persons, living or dead, or historical events, is purely coincidental.

First published by AuthorHouse 2/10/2006

ISBN: 1-4259-0326-6 (sc)

Printed in the United States of America
Bloomington, Indiana

This book is printed on acid-free paper.

Promenade - noun: a place for a leisurely walk

With a few exceptions

Table Of Contents

Prologue

The Bronx, New York City

A shabby store-lined pedestrian mall linked the elevated platforms of the New York City Transit System that dominated Jerome Avenue at 176th Street to surviving tenements on Davidson Avenue. Drugs, crime, and neglect infested the mall, perhaps envisioned as a neighborhood center, even a promenade, by city planners. The steel-shuttered doors of the closed shops became canvasses for local "artists." Spray-can Renoirs graffitied sides of buildings, walls, steps, and facings and sidewalks, concrete or brick, in a dizzying array of colors and gangland epithets.

Seventy-five crumbling steps led up from the promenade to Davidson Avenue.

The Jerome Deli, one of the promenade's survivors, sat on the corner of the mall and the avenue. The store announced its presence to the locals with a blue and yellow awning. A string of mini-flags from every Latin-American country flapped briskly under the awning. Crammed inside the small store was almost every item needed in this downtrodden neighborhood: food, telephone cards, an ATM, the New York Lotto, cigarettes.

"Mrs. Owens, what can I do for you today?" asked Raul Lopez, the owner of the bodega. Lopez, one of the few storeowners not driven out by despair, needed every customer he could get no matter how small their purchase or small their means. Three robberies in the last four months tested his faith.

Gwendolyn Owens, an asthmatic grandmother of sixty-three years, lived on Davidson Avenue, up those seventy-five steps that were to her a personal Everest. Today, she looked like she always did—black shoes, black dress, and a black lace Sunday church headpiece.

"I just need the milk and bread today." Owens' raspy voice from years of heavy smoking was barely audible.

"Trying to quit, right? No smokes then?"

Owens managed a nod as she clutched a loaf of Wonder Bread.

A genuine concern crossed Lopez's face. "I can always run something up to you if need be. I hope you know that, Mrs. Owens."

Again, there was only a nod. Owens was saving all her breath and dwindling energy for those stairs. She fumbled for a few dollars and paid the bill. She exited the grocery store and turned left. She took careful and measured steps as she crossed the brick-paved promenade. She came to the foot of the stairs. She paused and eyed the climb. She took a deep breath. With the small plastic bag holding milk and bread in her right hand and with her black purse hanging from her left wrist, she began the ascent. Her fatty left arm clutched the black, rusted pipe railing. The purse scraped along the pipe. Owens' tiny legs wobbled and buckled under her 200-pound, five-foot frame. It would take her a long time to reach the top. She rested at each of the five landings along the way.

She was slow. However, she was observant, an attentive spectator of the entire promenade and what it had to offer.

At times, that would include murder.

Chapter 1
"It's Par for the Course"

The third week of August would prove to be hot and humid along the eastern coast of the United States. It was Monday in the Bronx, New York. Joe MacLean, age thirty-six, a gold shield New York City detective assigned to the night shift out of the Bronx's 44th precinct, also known as the Bronx Task Force (BXTF), was sipping his fourth cup of Arabian Mocha coffee he bought by the pound at Starbucks. *Less than two hours left in this shift*, he thought. The station house brew tasted like shit so every week, he secured a one-pound bag in his desk. *Tasteful in small things; tasteful in all things.* It was Joe's personal motto.

The mini coffeemaker on the two-drawer file chirped annoyingly as Joe sipped from his Metropolitan Museum souvenir mug and began to leaf through the files on his desk. Recent homicides were on one pile and older, colder cases in a disorganized pile that threatened to creep onto his partner's desk alongside his.

Joe stretched and flicked off the coffeemaker and looked up. His partner, Hal, was thumbing through the folders in the black four-drawer file opposite the detectives' desks. Hal's half-eaten sandwich rested on top of the file cabinet. Joe thought he saw mayo on the file. Hal was forty-one and fat with an ample belly and fair skin with a touch of rosacea and green-eyed with light brown hair. Hal looked every inch like the stereotypical Irish cop. Nicknamed "Blimp" for his prodigious consumption of Blimpies' subs, Hal was ticking off the days to retirement, a heart attack, or both.

Despite his slovenliness, Hal was a good, solid officer, maybe not imaginative like Joe, but always the first through the door and always guarding his back. Hal had a dozen ribbons for valor, which he kept forgotten in a box in his precinct closet. Joe smiled inwardly when he thought of how often his older partner had saved his ass.

Joe was physically the complete opposite. Tall and trim, he kept in shape with daily workouts at the gym near his home. Where Hal had the crew-cut look, Joe wore his dark hair longer and combed straight back, looking like coach Pat Riley or like Al Pacino in *Scent of a Woman*.

Still handsome with dark Scotch-Irish looks, Joe wondered how long before the stress of the job ate away at his youthfulness. How long until he looked like Hal who was six years older. Depressed now, Joe pulled another slug of coffee as his thoughts switched to the domestic front.

His wife, Elizabeth, was on him to change over to the day shift, operating under the illusion that it was safer. Joe knew people got blown away at all hours but he humored her by telling her he would try to speak to the chief about a transfer to the seven to three haul, where Joe had originally begun in the motorcycle patrol. Blimp would have to transfer, too, and Joe knew that would probably never happen. They had spent three years together. He wanted to spend his nights at home in Rockland County, playing with his two kids, Jenna, eight, and Cory, four, and being with his wife who he still thought was as pretty and sexy as the day he met her.

The evening of Monday, August 18, in New York was especially hot and sticky. The sweat on Joe's forehead beaded like tiny jewels. The temperature had hit ninety-six at 3:00 p.m. It had been quiet for the past few evenings with no new homicides for Joe and Hal. The partners found themselves working on an old case still unsolved. *If only people would help the police with any kind of a lead,* Joe had thought often of how too many neighborhoods closed their eyes and plugged their ears to violence. The collective shame from the Kitty Genovese murder in March 1964 had long faded like a page in an old book. Assigning more detectives to a murder case for quicker resolution, Blimp said in his frequent retort to the chief, was like asking for Taj Mahal upgrades to the dumpy gray stone precinct that looked like an isolated fortress at the bottom of one of the many Bronx hills.

Hal grunted, breaking Joe out of his domestic reverie.

"What now?" Joe said.

"Fucking hot." Hal snorted.

"If you weren't so chunky, you would be cooler," Joe replied.

"Fuck you, sonny." Hal spoke without rancor.

"Just saying."

It was one of several well-practiced exchanges.

Hal walked over with a file on a rape and murder victim that had occurred on Jerome Avenue near the elevated train station. He stood dispirited in front of Joe's old but massive and useful oak desk.

"Shit, Joe, this gal didn't get raped and stabbed without anyone hearing or seeing the attack."

"It's par for the course." Joe sounded resigned.

Chapter 2
Beautiful By Her Early Teens

The heat wave stifling New York reached Paris on Tuesday afternoon. Dashing to the Air France terminal at DeGualle airport, Angela Aquino recalled how she had planned this vacation to New York for several months. She wanted to surprise a host of relatives on her late mother's side of the family. The relatives did not know she was coming. She had not seen the Valencia family since childhood when she left the Philippines and immigrated with her older sister and parents to Stuttgart, Germany. The Valencias had gone to New York City some years later and settled in the Bronx.

Scheduled takeoff time for the Air France Boeing 777-200 Flight 242 was 3:30 p.m. Paris time. Anticipated time of arrival for Angela and some additional 195 passengers at Newark Liberty International was 4:15 p.m. Eastern Standard Time.

Angela's vacation was part of her fortieth birthday celebration. She hoped to party with the Valencias the day after her arrival. Petite of build at five foot three and 105 pounds with black hair and brown eyes, Angela's good looks turned heads wherever she went.

Beautiful by her early teens, Angela took after her mother, Josephine. Josephine was Miss Queson City of 1958. It was at age seven that Angela, her full name being Maria Angela, immigrated with her older sister, Maria Patricia, then eleven, and with their parents, Leon and Josephine.

The family moved to Germany when a prominent auto executive from Porsche AG promised Leon Aquino work in the design/research division of the then fledging sports car manufacturer. That was in 1969. There had not been much work for someone like Leon Aquino in the Philippines. He enjoyed designing cars but was willing, though, to do any work as long as it had to do with automobiles. Since childhood, Leon had designed automobiles. Most of his jobs in the Philippines focused on auto repairs. With no major manufacturers of automobiles in the Philippines, there was no need for designers.

However, Leon Aquino struck gold that spring of '69. In Stuttgart, Germany, corporate headquarters of Porsche AG, auto executive Hans Becker received many job résumés. He took an interest nonetheless in the Filipino's original ideas, evident in Leon's portfolio of designs. After clearing it with the headman, Becker offered Leon a position in the company. He admitted to associates, although not to his superior, it might be clever to offer a beginning design position to an Asian. After all, there were some good designs at the time emerging from Pacific Rim companies such as Datsun and Toyota. Perhaps this Philippine could be a true diamond in the rough, reflected Becker.

As fate would have it, their father's association with Hans Becker would influence Angela and Patricia for good and for bad.

Now it was 2002. Angela walked briskly through the terminal dressed in a loose-fitting and simple above-the-knee, cap-sleeve chestnut brown dress with brown cloth buttons and mandarin collar. She clutched tightly her small color-coordinated carryon bag. The bag held precious photos of both her late father and mother never seen before by the relatives in the Bronx.

With Papa Aquino's death, his daughters came into money back in Stuttgart. With the inheritance and a generous amount of money Hans Becker gave to Angela, the two sisters opened the Spa at San Agustin, Canary Islands, in 1991. Angela and Patricia's fluency in Spanish, German, and English proved an important benefit at the spa that catered to wealthy vacationers from all over the world but especially continental Europe.

Besides the photos of her late parents, Angela's carryon also held a dozen choice handmade cigars from the Canary

Islands, the archipelago of eternal springtime, where Angela and Patricia operated the full-service spa.

"Uncle Jose loves cigars. Why don't you surprise him with some 'Puros de la Palma,'" said Patricia a few days before Angela left Gran Canaria, the third largest of the Canary Islands and export home of the islands' tobacco industry. Canarians rate with some of the world's best cigars, very expensive to purchase in the USA at about $10.00 per cigar. Angela selected Penamil Gran Reserva for Uncle Jose.

As Angela hurried through the terminal, her small brown leather purse swayed back and forth on her right shoulder. The purse held the usual stuff and the address of the Valencia family in the Bronx. Angela breathed a sigh of relief as she spotted the Air France departure gate number 141.

But Angela carried something else. Her body embraced money, Euros, cleverly hidden into an oversized bra. The loose-fitting clothes concealed most of Angela's curves. Her breasts were a cup size larger than usual because of the concealed money. A cardigan sweater of navy blue spotted with the mountain laurel blossom, the representative flower of the Canary Islands, helped cover her exaggerated bosom as well as her shoulders and arms. Patricia gave the handmade sweater to Angela just before her departure.

"Never know about the weather!" said her sister believing the climate in the USA could not be as perfect as the astonishingly pleasant and consistent temperatures of the Canary Islands.

Much to Angela's chagrin, the concealed Euros would soon play center stage in the lives of other passengers aboard the Air France flight.

Also scheduled to take off that afternoon from Paris were Barbara and Cliff Neldon, fifty-nine and sixty respectively; Ben Davis, Arthur Katz, and Beatrice (Trixie) Jurgens, all sixty-four and all returning from a ten-day cruise through the Western Mediterranean. For these five travelers, Charles DeGualle Airport was the second leg after the one-hour-fifteen-minute flight from Rome. Ben, Art, and Trixie were college chums, class of '60, while Art knew Cliff from their years of working together as school administrators in New Jersey. All now had more time and resources to travel. For Barbara and Cliff, it was a first cruise. For the college friends, it was another excursion on their long list. The weather for this recent cruise that began in Barcelona with stops in Cannes, Porto Fino, and Monaco and finally Rome, had been perfect, unusual for August in the Mediterranean.

As the departure time drew closer, DeGualle airport's colossal paneled-glass dome spreading over the terminal like a phoenix watched and quietly laughed at the humdrum below. Experienced airline travelers called DeGualle one of the ugliest and most confusing places in the airline industry. Only after several frenzied inquiries, Angela finally reached the departure gate. She eyed the departure time. She took a deep breath. The beautiful Angela had charmed her way through French customs.

At least for now, the Euros hidden in her bra did not set off any alarms.

Chapter 3
"Incommunicado"

Angela had twenty minutes to gather her thoughts before the scheduled departure. She recalled that in 1980, when Angela was only eighteen, Hans Becker was thirty-eight. Papa Leon did fulfill his dream with opportunities to work on some designs. His death, however, in 1980, left the family with no significant breadwinner other than Patricia who brought in some money working in customer service for a German bank. Hans then offered Angela a secretarial position at Porsche AG in Stuttgart. Angela, a take-your-breath-away beauty, resisted the advances of Hans Becker who had more in mind than a working relationship. Angela's strict Catholic upbringing told her to stay away from the married Hans.

At least this would be the excuse for a while.

Now, Angela could only think of a relaxing vacation. She was excited about flying off to America. Her restlessness prompted a question of the Air France attendant at the boarding station.

"How much longer?"

"We should be boarding the plane in ten to twelve minutes, Mademoiselle."

Angela took a seat among the contoured gray plastic benches a few yards from the boarding station. Across from Angela, Barbara and Cliff found some empty seats. Cliff removed the bookmark in Eco's *Baudalino* and began to read. Fumbling through her purse, Barbara reassured herself for at least the third or fourth time that the boarding passes were in order. Angela made brief eye contact with Barbara, the kind of person who started a conversation with anyone, often to Cliff's consternation. He often lamented,

"Why would they be interested in our trivia?" or Barbara's way of beginning a conversation. For the moment, Barbara settled for boarding pass assurance, eye contact, and a brief smile in the direction of Angela.

Angela fidgeted. The money hidden in her bra made for an uncomfortable fit. She had decided the hidden money required a larger bra cup. Now, however, Angela could not shed her self-consciousness at 36C rather than 34B. In hiding the money, she saw no dishonesty. She did not want US Customs to know about the Euros. Most of the money was a cash gift to the Valencia family. Patricia had said that Aunt Valencia's family was not as well off as they were. With cash, no one would ask the Valencias to explain a few new comforts. Angela smiled inwardly thinking of the generosity.

Angela reached into her purse to glance once again at the Bronx address, 1727 Davidson Avenue between 175th Street and 176th Street. *What kind of neighborhood is it?*

Angela daydreamed. After her visit to the Valencias, who were not expecting a visit from this far-off niece,

Angela planned to see the sights—Manhattan, Washington D.C., perhaps other locations. She decided on a return to the Canary Islands via Barcelona by late September after spending three business days in the Spanish city. She had already stopped in Paris for several days before her departure to America, marketing the spa to corporate executives.

Patricia, ordinary in appearance compared to Angela, and Patricia's husband, Erik, ran the day-to-day operations of the Spa at San Agustin on Gran Canaria's tourist-centered eastern coast. The saucer-shaped island is an almost perfectly circular-shaped land mass with the spa on the east coast about thirty-three miles south of Las Palmas, the provincial capital located nearly at the northern top of Gran Canaria. Angela had promised her sister she would return by late September because business at the spa perked up with the first chill in Europe. Only her sister knew her plans. She did not want Hans or any of her friends to know. "Incommunicado" was the way Angela saw her vacation. "Peace and quiet," she had insisted.

"And please, I truly want to surprise Maria and Jose. Tell no one. The money will help them."

"And don't tell Erik either!" Angela never liked Erik. The feeling was mutual.

Chapter 4
Warm Beaches

It was the summer of 1990. The winter of '89-90 had been bitterly cold in major parts of Europe. Stuttgart, within a short distance from the Swabian Alps, suffered the worst of it. Close to 120 inches of snow fell and the citizens endured several zero-degree days. The winter enthusiasts could not be happier with the nearby Alps resembling dark chocolate cakes piled high with mounds of white fluffy frosting.

Angela hated the cold. This was not the climate of her early youth in the Philippines. She longed for warm ocean breezes. Angela was now twenty-eight with an exquisite figure. She dreamed of lying on warm beaches with sand between her toes. Angela was sexually reserved but had been intimate with Hans, his Teutonic goods looks and wealth making him hard to resist. These liaisons were secret of course. If his wife knew of the affair, Hans faced ruin with a messy divorce, loss of prestige within the conservative-thinking company where he was now the number three executive, and alimony. Hans, secretly generous, made Angela's lifestyle more lavish than her secretarial salary allowed. Without Hans, but because of his money, Angela took a vacation in the summer of 1990 to Spain's playground—the Canary Islands.

Ahh…warm beaches!

The Canary Islands were a tropical paradise. After landing at the airport on Gran Canaria, Angela flagged a yellow Fiat taxi with a blue roof. The cab had seen better days, the front bumper amply dented and reflecting the bright Atlantic sun in a myriad of angles.

Grand Canaria was the major island among the seven uniquely different isles that hugged the coast of North

Africa and comprised the archipelago. Tenerife, Lanzorote, and Gran Canaria were the largest of the seven islands.

Angela's first views astonished her. From the cab's right rear window, Angela could see the island's sparkling beaches warmed by the Canaries current. However, as she glanced to her left, she saw highlands and mountains covered with snow. She had read up on the history: The islands were colonized by the Spaniards around the time of Columbus (indeed, Columbus had used Gran Canaria as a rest stop on his way to New World discoveries), called idyllic and enchanting by the ancients such as Herodotus and Homer, while Pliny labeled them the Fortunate Isles. Most fascinating of all said some, these volcanic isles represented the tips of the lost continent of Atlantis. Angela had read too about the variety of vegetation from sub-tropical to volcanic semi-deserts, from green-covered cliffs and gorges to endless sand dunes reaching to the sea.

Angela sat back as comfortably as she could in the taxi's small back seat. In the cab's rearview mirror, Angela fixated for the moment on the young cabby's blue eyes. *He's kind of cute.*

Today, Angela wore a multicolored V-neck shirt blouse with knee-length white pants slit at the knee and adorned with red buttons.

As the taxi reached Las Palmas, meaning City of Palms, about fifteen miles north of the airport, the beach called Playa de las Canteras came into view. It was almost three miles long. The Atlantic waves broke gently on its golden beach. Any force was spent crashing over a natural breakwater reef. Swimmers and sunbathers were everywhere. The Avenida Maritima, a promenade for lazy strolls among quaint shops and cafés, ran the entire length of the beach. Angela spotted, off to the left of the cab, one of the many parks of Las Palmas, the Santa Catalina Park with its bountiful variety of flowers. Angela saw her favorites— violets and chrysanthemums. Las Palmas boasted almost 400,000 residents, having spread far beyond the old city of Vegueta-Triana.

As the taxi plodded along the narrow streets, the old city came into view. Flowers were everywhere, reaching colorfully far beyond the open spaces and parks. Flowers and plants hung spider-like from black iron-railed Andalusian-style balconies of the many white stucco Moorish-style apartments. Saffron, pink, mauve, violet, light blue, purple, yellow, cream-colored, and white were just a sampling of the colors. Fragrance filled the taxi as air rushed through the cab's four open windows.

Angela had arrived on islands famous for flowers. The isles were of great botanical interest. Here grew chrysanthemums, lilies, daffodils, and snowdrops, iris, rush, orchids, geraniums, hibiscus, pansies, and violets. Aromatic shrubs abounded such as the artemisia and holly; many varieties of trees including the olive and jasmine, elder, Canarian willow, Tamadaba pines, and the mountain laurel were largely exploited and found mostly in the valley known as Los Tiles de Maya on the eastern coast. Ground cover included the pink or white cineraria, with walls covered by the mauve-flowered canarienis. Rarest of all were the endemic "dragon trees," or dracaena with one wide solid trunk and tens upon tens of sky-reaching branches sprouting from thirty to fifty feet from the top of the main shaft like an ancient Hydra. Flowers had always played a big role in Canarian history as food, shelter, forage, and medicine. Today, flowers are a major export.

"This is so lovely. Is it always this full of flowers and fragrance?"

Angela again eyed the cabby, a nice-looking young man who she guessed to be about twenty-five.

During the twenty-minute drive, the cabby had taken several long looks in his rearview mirror at the beauty that had chosen his cab as if it were an honor. *She is stunning!* When he did manage to look ahead at traffic, he leaned unmercifully on the horn, bullying private cars, other taxis, mopeds, and bicycles out of his way.

The cabby spoke in competent English.

"This is nothing compared to the feast of Corpus Christi in late May when the whole city is decked out—carpets of flowers. The residents compete for the most beautiful arrangements of flower petals. It is a decades-old tradition. The streets are a parade of colors."

"My, that sounds wonderful. And the city—what would you recommend seeing?"

"There's lots, señorita. Mind you, this is not Madrid or Barcelona, but we have nice museums, shops, and you must see over there (the young man pointed to his right) in the old town, the Cathedral de Santa Ana in the gothic and Catalonian style."

The young man paused, thinking of the pretty woman in his cab. "And the beaches, you have your swimwear— maybe bikini?"

Angela ignored the intent of the question. "Tell me more about the cathedral!"

"Well, first of all, during that holiday, Corpus Christi I mentioned, the palazzo in front of the cathedral is full of the flower carpets. It was for me especially wonderful to see as a child, so many beautiful designs—religious years ago but now, not so much. Not only flowers but also seeds to make the designs."

"And the cathedral itself?"

"I believe they call it classical. It took 400 years to build!"

"Ah, that sounds like something you'd find in Rome."

The cabby spoke proudly.

"Roman columns outside but with a gothic ceiling. Outside three distinctive horizontal levels as you look from the palazzo. On the top level, two bell towers on opposite sides and a throne-like arch in the center. In the middle, a beautiful rose window with an entrance of three magnificent arches. I think you will like it. You don't have to be religious, you know."

"Yes, well that style is neoclassical. And inside?"

"Again, very beautiful. Simple in light green and white, gold relief on the many arches and columns. I like especially the lantern-style lights that give the cathedral a warm atmosphere."

"Sounds much like the typical ascetic churches you find in Spain."

The driver continued to pay little attention to speed as he whizzed through the streets. He had already been racing from the airport on the Gran Canaria 1 Highway, dubbed GC 1.

"Do you always drive so fast?"

"I want to get you to the hotel in quick time," asserted the cabby as he swerved to avoid still another moped.

"And, señorita, let me warn you."

"Warn me? About what?"

"Whistling. Men whistle...but here it is a common way of communication...to overcome the steep terrain in certain places. If you go to the beautiful and scenic ravines, shouting is no good. They whistle to get another's attention." A happy expression filled his youthful face.

"Well, thank you for warning me. So I shouldn't expect too many compliments?"

"I didn't say that, señorita." Angela took notice of the cabby's broad smile glittering in the rearview mirror.

The fresh air of the island had Angela's thoughts drifting again. She could not stomach the airline food. Hunger made Angela think of food. She hoped to bring back some of the famous recipes of the Canaries that combined traditional Spanish with African and Latin-American influences. Plenty of fish, especially hake, were caught in large amounts along the coast; it was most often made with mojo, a hot sauce of oil, garlic, chili peppers, and paprika. Angela had heard also about the good local wines, Canarian rum, and excellent desserts such as Platanos Fritos or fried bananas. Bananas grew well in the volcanic soil and semi-tropical climate resulting in the island's famous sweet banana liqueur. Also grown here were papayas, mangoes, and avocadoes.

Angela also looked forward to seeing more of the spectacular scenery. The shape of Gran Canaria was like a wheel with deep ravines called barrancos comprising the spokes and radiating from the center of the island. Volcanic monoliths abounded making the island a geologist's paradise.

"We will be there in just a few minutes," said the driver.

During the five-mile journey within Las Palmas, the taxi passed stately old homes in the traditional white stucco design but also three- or four-storied apartments and their typical black-iron balconies overlooking grand pedestrian esplanades. The terraces proved great visages from which the residents observed tourists as well as kept a watchful eye on the comings and goings of the locals.

"Besides the cathedral, señorita," said the cabby, "you will want to go see the Columbus House. We call it Casa Museo Colon. It is a museum about the times of Columbus. And the natives of these islands, they were called Guanches, you can learn about them, too, at the museum. The museum has some skulls to prove it!"

The cab driver smiled and lifted his eyes to the rearview mirror.

The cabby rushed his words, "Ah, we are almost there, another kilometer. There is dancing and singing every Thursday and Sunday in Doramus Park, very beautiful. We enjoy salsa music here...lots of Cuban influence on our music and food. The Santa Catalina casino is there, too."

"I don't plan to gamble."

"And stay out of some of the seedy sections. After all, Las Palmas has many citizens and not all are so nice like me. The hotel will assist you as to where not to go."

"Thank you so much for the information." Angela spotted a blue and white sign shaped like a shield that announced the Hotel de la Carla was one-half kilometer.

At first sight, Angela found the resort disappointing. A frown temporarily marred Angela's pretty face. The wood-framed Victorian-style main building painted blue with taupe trim was in good condition but needed fresh paint. *After all, brochures always make a place look its best.*

As the taxi managed the sharp incline to the hotel's entrance, the overworked and in-need-of-an-oil-change engine left a flume like a black cloud in its wake.

The hotel's grounds, thought Angela, appeared pleasant enough despite some tall grass and weeds along the concrete driveway. The hedges on both sides of the driveway were neatly trimmed. Lime trees dotted the landscape to the left and right of the driveway. A forest of Tamadaba pines, native to the islands, stood thick off to the far left of the Hotel de la Carla's entrance. To the far right, recreation areas consisting of a pool, tennis courts, and miniature golf found vacationers enjoying the warm sunshine.

The taxi chugged up the hill, coming to a merciful rest under the hotel's carriageway entrance. In years past, horses and buggies or coaches with uniformed drivers would have brought many of Grand Canaria's richest, most bejeweled, most elegant citizens to the hotel. After stepping away from the horse and carriage, the rich and famous would then have paraded on a red carpet leading up the wide stairs to the grand entrance hall.

Those days were long gone.

Angela tipped the driver and said with mild sarcasm, "Here, I hope you get an oil change soon!"

The young cabby nodded and took one more long, last stare at Angela.

The four-storied Victorian hotel welcomed arrivals with a large porch on three sides of the building. For taking in the views of the pine forest in the distance and the great lawn in the foreground, wicker chairs and rockers lined the railed porticos. A big but friendly golden retriever greeted Angela at the top of the wooden, gray-painted stairs, wagging its tail merrily. Angela managed two moderate-sized pieces of luggage through the front screen door. The entrance hall still had the aura of the grand old days. Mahogany ruled: chairs with comfortable-looking green upholstery encircled the reception area, a plush divan, an armoire and two chests of drawers added more richness. A chandelier illuminated the circular hall and directed visitors to the registration desk to the immediate left.

Angela was happy again. *The place is charming inside!* Angela assumed perhaps it was not, given some of the dull paint outside. After signing in, she made her way to her room on the third floor.

The corner room proved delightful: soft yellow walls with sage-colored and flowered window treatments on the one small double-hung window overlooked the lush pine forest. A large sliding door led to the spacious and welcoming balcony. A king-size canopied bed with a room-matching yellow and sage bedspread, an oak writing table and dresser, two inviting upholstered chairs, and a reading table all sat on a plush tan carpet. Locally fired pottery decorated the room. A basket made of palm leaves, reed, and wicker added visual pleasure to the reading table. Delicate white embroidery, probably local too, thought Angela, adorned the dresser.

Angela opened the sliding door and stepped onto the balcony. *The ocean looks magnificent. The coast of Morocco, only about seventy miles distant.* Angela reached up and fixed her long black hair as a gentle breeze swept over the veranda.

Angela had booked a week of relaxation at the hotel; no word processors, no phones, no rude calls from those American Porsche dealers saying the company needed to ship the hot Boxsters faster to demanding buyers, moreover, no groping hands of Hans Becker.

The sojourn would change Angela for the rest of her life.

Chapter 5
BXTF

"Hal, I think we may have caught a break in this rape and murder case up on Jerome."

Hal had just entered the second-floor office at BXTF. Joe was leafing through a report from forensics. Hal muttered a series of his usual complaints, appearing not to have heard Joe.

"Goddamn heat!" Then…

"Shitty precinct." Louder…

"Fucking sick of fast food. Need some of Linda's home-cooking for a change." Brazenly…

"We got something useful from the glorified asses in forensics?"

Hal slammed an open file closed, taking enjoyment in the finality of the action.

Joe figured Hal was jealous with the TV shows exaggerating sexy aspects of police work. The beat cop and even the homicide detective had disappeared from the nightly line-up. Everything was DNA, CSI, and forensics!

"It says here we have a DNA match with a guy now at Rikers." Joe spoke with mild excitement hoping Hal would share in the good news.

"Maybe, Hal, this case will be resolved after all."

Hal lowered the tone of his voice but kept up the sarcasm. "Great, those namby-pamby geneticists can solve all the crimes." Hal glanced at the wall clock: 10:30 p.m. give or take a few ticks.

Hal shuffled toward Joe.

"Maybe those fruits can get some improvements to this place."

Hal stared down at the scuffed and marred black-and-white tiled floor. He plopped down in a squeaky and torn hunter green swivel chair opposite Joe's desk. Hal began to calm down as he peered around the twelve-by-sixteen second-floor office partitioned off from the records room and a few more nondescript offices manned by robbery and narcotics.

"What's up, Joe?" Hal was now focused and anxious to move on with the eight-month-old case.

"Chief Brennan says we need to interview this guy first thing tomorrow." Then after a moment's pause…

"Jesus, Mary, Joseph, that's only eight-plus hours from now." Joe's voice mirrored a dispirited attitude as he shed the slouch and straightened up in the chair.

"We may have to go on days with this case for a while, Hal."

"Shit," said Hal.

Joe stood up, yawned loudly, and stretched upward toward the ceiling. "Let's get home and get some sleep."

Hal blasted several farts as he pushed the swivel chair back into a corner.

"Fast food, whatta ya expect?"

"Christ, what a stink!"

Joe closed the old wide-style wooden blinds. Hal shut the lights by pushing the ancient-style black button. They exited the office. They worked the steps down from the second floor of the precinct/task force. The stairwell was oppressively hot with no windows or ventilation. A lousy paint job was evident with spots of gray paint here and there on the metal steps. Even the aluminum railing, usually cool to the touch, seemed warm under these humid conditions.

"Jesus, my boxers are sticking to my ass," grumbled Blimp.

"Adios, Amigo...hasta luego." Joe waved to the night desk sergeant as he and Hal hastened through the front door of the precinct station. Lopsidedly fastened over the front door and under the nearly opaque half-moon window, hung the crudely scripted "BXTF." Only nailed to the crossbeam above the wooden door, some cops said it was an appropriate reminder of the crucifixion.

The next day would be Tuesday, August 19. The weather girls were claiming the heat wave would break with light rain probable by late afternoon. For the moment, Joe hoped for a breeze to whisk away the fumes of the city as he and Hal headed for the high-fenced parking yard and their cars. Traffic rumbled by on the nearby Major Deegan Expressway only the width of the street and a sloping 200 yards below.

Joe said goodbye to Hal who unlocked his red Ford Explorer and checked for any new pings and dents. He was obsessive about the condition of his SUV. Hal lived out in Selden, Long Island, and a two-hour drive away in bad traffic. Hal hoped to make it in less than ninety minutes.

Joe slipped behind the wheel of his green '99 Volkswagen Jetta. Intense fatigue overcame him. *My god, I have to clean this car soon.* Joe removed a few TastyKake wrappers from the dash and tossed them on the passenger-side floor already littered with paper coffee cups and part of yesterday's snack food binge. Joe always had a weakness for desserts, if you could call junk food dessert. His excuse? Mom always said, "No dessert unless you eat your vegetables."

Joe called them "forgettables!"

The BXTF was eerily isolated. The Major Deegan Expressway ran along the Harlem River. Not far to the south was Yankee Stadium. New York City's oldest bridge, the pedestrian High Bridge or Poe Bridge connected upper Manhattan with the Bronx and traversed the Harlem River to the north. The bridge resembled a Roman aqueduct with its multiple archways. It was indeed a conduit in the nineteenth century, carrying fresh water from the Croton River in Westchester County to reservoirs in Central Park. It was also called the Poe Bridge. Edgar Allan Poe reportedly composed his remorseful poem "Annabelle Lee" on the bridge when he lived for a short time in the Bronx.

Joe had many interests, tasteful interests, he believed. He admired Poe's work and relished the history of New York City and the borough of the Bronx. He also found irresistible Broadway show tunes, especially those of the 1950s and 1960s.

BXTF, situated at the bottom of one of the many Bronx hills, gave Joe fits during winter's ice and snow. His car always slid down the hill coming to the station or struggled up the hill when he needed to escape for home. BXTF stood as an outpost, distant from other buildings and very different contrasted to the densely packed borough with its crowded streets. High fences topped with barbwire protected the officers' cars from roaming street kids. You still had to sidestep the broken bottles and make certain you did not run over twisted metal driving out of the parking yard.

As this moment amid his fatigue—*Thank God it is only a hop and skip to the George Washington Bridge, then the Palisades Interstate Parkway and home.* Home was Garnerville, Rockland County, New York. Joe and Liz purchased the ten-room colonial three years ago from a dentist who had relocated to Connecticut. He recalled the Remax ad, "Lovely four-bedroom, spacious family room, 2½-bath home with large kitchen, newer carpeting, deck and pool, and two-car garage on spacious lot in nice neighborhood." Joe still had to invest thousands into the house beginning with a remodeled kitchen, outside paint, some landscaping improvements, and a new pump and filter for the pool. It was a quiet neighborhood and a good place to raise the kids. Another cop lived down the block with his wife, a narcotics unit guy out of Manhattan, but he was not that friendly, perhaps even jealous—*Liz is prettier. That must be it.*

At this hour, 11:30 p.m., earlier than even the usual quitting time for Joe, the travel was already easy on the Palisades Interstate Parkway. Light traffic was at least one advantage of working the night shift 4 to 12. Joe sighted Exit 14 as he turned down the car's Alpine CD player. Joe loved the old Broadway musicals and was listening tonight to Rogers and Hammerstein. The vintage melodies always raced through his mind. Sometimes, the tunes distracted him from the intense thinking required of homicide detectives.

Elizabeth was already in bed and the kids were fast asleep when Joe quietly unlocked the front door at about midnight. He peeked in on the kids. All was precious. Liz more often than not waited up for Joe, but today had been more exhausting than usual. She had taken the kids to the Bronx Zoo. Joe could only imagine the smells in the gorilla building, the piles of dung in the elephants' enclave, the squawking, loud cranes in the aviary. Zoos were not Joe's favorite place once you got past the cute pandas.

Joe wanted to tell Liz about the shift to days. *It may only be for this case and a few days or a few weeks at best but still, she would welcome the change.* Liz was sound asleep. He decided that if she didn't hear him get up in the morning, shower and shave, get dressed *etcetera, etcetera, etcetera,* Joe recalled the *King and I,* one of his favorites, he'd leave her a big note on the breakfast counter under the salt and pepper shakers and definitely call her on the cell the next day.

He hoped she would be happy with the change. *Shall we dance, shall we dance, shall we dance*...and other catchy melodies from the Yul Bryner/Deborah Kerr version echoed in Joe's thoughts as he snuggled next to Liz, kissed her blonde hair, and dosed off.

Chapter 6
Bonjour

Back in Paris, first-class passengers heard the announcement in French then in English to board Air France Flight A242. Barbara and Cliff began to collect their bags. Barbara, slender for her age, dressed in a simple orange blouse and white slacks. Cliff struggled with a middle gut. According to their friends, Barbara and Cliff often wore the same color combinations. It was never planned, it just worked out that way. That was what Cliff told their travel companions as they noticed Cliff's beige khakis and orange pullover.

Ben, Art, and Trixie boarded first, having seats near the rear of the plane three abreast in row 42. Ben, a diminutive five feet eight and 140 pounds with a good head of black hair making him look younger than his years, took the window seat. Arthur, short, stocky, and partly bald, sat in the middle seat, and Trixie, tall and big-boned with a gimpy leg eased into the aisle seat. The travel agent had screwed up Cliff and Barbara's seating, they were not near their travel companions nor were they assigned seats together. The Air France agent at the gate had said to board the plane first and then ask someone to switch seats.

Within a few minutes, coach passengers on the canopy-covered gangway filed into the plane. They received the customary "Welcome aboard, Bonjour Mademoiselle, Monsieur," from the flight attendants in their blue-with-white-trim Air France uniforms.

Angela boarded and took a seat next to the window in row 32, two rows behind the emergency exit doors. As Barbara discovered row 32 seat B, Cliff tossed the carryon bags into the overhead compartments. Cliff found his assigned seat a few rows back. All the seats including those of their travel companions were on the left side of the plane. The middle aisle sat four and then there were three seats on the opposite side.

"Hello." Barbara recognized the woman from the terminal as she adjusted her clothing to the contours of the seat. Angela, already a true Canarian famous for their friendly and seemingly endless good disposition, replied with a soft "Hello" in response.

"Is this seat empty?" Barbara referred to seat C on the aisle.

"I know it's not for anyone with me, I'm traveling alone," Angela answered in a stronger, more forceful voice this time as the din of the passengers still finding their seats engulfed the area. Just then, a portly man sat down in seat C on the aisle. Barbara shifted her shoulders back and forth. She felt uneasy with the strange man next to her and Cliff a few rows behind.

The female flight attendant promptly came over to the man in seat C and asked him first in French and then, after a blank stare, repeated in English if he would kindly move to seat 40C where Cliff was waiting so a husband and wife could sit together.

"No problem as long as it's another seat on the aisle," declared the round-faced American man as he began to shift to a new seat. "You know that commercial, the one that has the jingle 'gotta go, gotta go, right now,' well that's yours truly!"

Barbara laughed, the flight attendant smiled, and Cliff noticed the attendant motioning him to move up to the seat next to his wife. Barbara thanked the man for his consideration. He nodded politely. Cliff arrived at his new seat, towering over the tiny flight attendant as he thanked her for her prompt attention to Barbara's request. Within a few seconds, Cliff slid into the seat next to Barbara.

"Cliff, take off your coat before you have to belt down." Barbara always worried about Cliff being too warm and thus becoming overheated with his high blood pressure problem.

"I'll be fine." Cliff would rather be warmer than colder.

"Oh boy," Cliff leaned slightly over in an appeal to Barbara's right ear, anxiously adding, "I hope the attendant doesn't pick me to open that emergency door in case of trouble." No one asked.

The takeoff went smoothly. Within moments, the suburbs of Paris came into view through the porthole-size windows. Angela, of course, had the best seat for viewing. Barbara and Cliff craned to see what they could.

Dinner was served within twenty minutes, choice of veal ragout or hake with tomato sauce. Mealtime gave Barbara a chance to begin small talk with Angela.

"Hello, my name is Barbara. Where are you headed to?"

"New York, the Bronx...My name is Angela, how do you do?"

"I am fine, thank you. You said the Bronx? I'm originally from Manhattan. Have you been to New York before?"

"No, I've never been to New York, never been to the United States."

"What brings you to America?

"Visiting...I am surprising relatives in the Bronx."

"Are you from France?"

"Ah no, I'm originally from the Philippines...lived in Germany for a while. I now live in the Canary Islands."

Barbara had been memorizing U.S. state capitals in a mental exercise and part contest with Cliff who had taken on the task of world capitals and had gotten down all of Europe's capital cities. "Keep the mind active," Barbara was saying. "We are not getting any younger."

Barbara shifted the veal and parslied rice around on her airline plastic plate, not certain if it looked appetizing. She did not feel particularly hungry. Happiness would have been a buttered roll and a cup of hot tea.

"Cliff, what's the capital of the Canary Islands?" Barbara turned away from the sight of the food.

"The Canary Islands? Why?" Cliff relished the hake on his plate.

Barbara looked at Cliff's plate. *How can he eat that stuff?*

"Just please tell me, Cliff."

Barbara has made a new friend. "Well, honey, the Canary Islands is part of Spain and the capital of Spain is Madrid." Cliff spoke robotically.

"I couldn't help but hear you ask about the Canaries," inquired Angela. "What would you like to know?"

"It must be beautiful," commented Barbara, "they are somewhere in the Atlantic Ocean, right?"

"Off the coast of Morocco."

"You mean Bogart, Casablanca, exotic music, French gendarmes looking like Claude Rains?" Barbara and Cliff had recently purchased several boxed sets of film classics. They had probably seen *Casablanca* ten times.

"That's right. The Canaries are about seventy miles off the coast of North Africa. My sister and I run a health spa, the Spa at San Agustin. Perhaps you and..." Angela leaned over to catch a glimpse of Cliff.

"I <u>am</u> sorry; this is Cliff, my husband. We are returning with friends, they are a few rows back, from a cruise, Barcelona to Rome. The weather was astonishingly good."

Angela and Cliff exchanged hellos.

"And I am Angela, how do you do?" Angela bowed her head slightly in the direction of Cliff.

Angela redirected her comments to Barbara.

"As I was saying, you and Cliff should consider the Canaries some day. Our weather is usually perfect—sixty-five to seventy-two degrees—a touch of humidity now and then, but perhaps the most consistent weather anywhere in the world. The climate, I understand, is like your weather in Central Florida. They are both the same latitude."

"Cliff, that sounds wonderful, doesn't it? We should talk to Art and ask him if he's been there. I don't think so, right?"

"No, no, and I'm sure Arty would have mentioned it." Cliff pondered...*I first need to pay for this trip before I can think of another and she has us going somewhere already.*

The flight attendant asked if anyone needed a refill on his or her drinks.

Barbara continued. "We will ask our travel companions. They are the world travelers. This was our first cruise although we have been to Europe, Rome in fact, before."

"I see."

"A spa, that sounds wonderful. A massage f-e-e-l-s sooo good." Barbara drew out the onomatopoeia as if it were a Poe masterpiece.

"We have a complete facility: massaging showers, sea mudpacks, whirlpools, and more. Massages are a part of it but you can swim, sun, hike, bicycle, and shop on the island. The sand is black where we are because of ancient volcanic activity, but the islands also have many white sand and golden sand beaches. Not to worry, the black sand is clean. Las Palmas is our capital. Gran Canaria, one of the largest of the islands, is where we are."

"Black sand? I've never heard of such a thing."

Barbara turned slightly directing her words to Cliff.

"Cliff, I thought you said the Canaries didn't have a capital?"

Cliff looked bewildered as he took a sip from his refilled cup of ginger ale.

"Las Palmas is only a provincial capital, Barbara, sorry to confuse the issue. It is like your state capitals in America."

Barbara recalled Angela's description of Canarian activities…

"Believe it or not, I never learned to ride a bike," said Barbara apologetically.

"In the city, you use public transportation…I'm a good swimmer, though. Spent many summers as a kid out on Far Rockaway, that's one of the beaches in New York…white sand by the way. My aunt and uncle had a bungalow out there."

"Beaches, in New York?"

"Yes, very nice, but too crowded nowadays and not very clean, I don't think. It's been years."

"Well, ours can be crowded, especially during the height of the tourist season. Several hundreds of thousands come to the Canaries when the weather turns cold in Europe. October through March is our busiest time."

Barbara continued reminiscing. "Those were nice times. The bungalows are long gone for high rises. Times change."

Angela picked up the sentiment. "Yes, they do."

The conversation lapsed for a several minutes. Angela stared out the window. Clouds now covered the western coast of France, gnawing the peaks of the Massif Range. Angela's face had the look of someone wanting to share a concern but not certain if it was the right thing to do.

Perhaps these people will know about customs in the U.S. Should I ask or not?

The concealed Euros had Angela blushing, if only inwardly—for now.

Chapter 7
Reflection

It was September 1990, Angela's sojourn to the Canary Islands.

This is one of the most beautiful locales in the world. Angela was 28. Her shapely figure absorbed the Canarian sun as she sunbathed on the golden sand beach of Maspalomas, about thirty-six miles down the eastern coast from Las Palmas. Playa del Ingles was a short distance to the north with two miles of white sand and a nude beach area. *Not for me, save nudity for the private places in our lives.* There were many ice cream vendors on the beaches and fast-food establishments just off the shore.

The Hotel de la Carla was comfortable but not exciting. Angela inquired about the best beaches. *Maspalomas is definitely one of them.* The sky blue bikini swimsuit revealed her well-tanned and attractive figure.

The waves from the Atlantic Ocean kissed the sandy beach. Angela rubbed more sun tan lotion on her legs and arms. *This is where I want to live! But how?* Angela saved most of her earnings and was a cautious spender of Hans' money. *Is it possible? With my savings from the inheritance, a loan, some cash from Hans, and perhaps help from Patricia, I can purchase the small spa that was for sale along the road on the way down here from Las Palmas. But...would Hans be a problem?* He was very possessive of Angela and enjoyed their moments of intimacy. *The Canary Islands are a long way from Stuttgart.*

She remembered, too, perhaps more wishfully than it deserved, that Patricia was not happy either living in the colder continental climate. *Neither of us...Heidi longing for the Alps!* Angela thought Patricia might be interested in a business venture if Patricia could convince the shiftless

Erik. Erik was twenty-seven and five years younger than Patricia and a year younger than Angela. *No ambition in that Erik!* Angela believed Erik was going nowhere, still being in security for the bank. That was when Patricia started dating Erik, when both were working for Deutches Bank. *What does Patricia see in Erik? Never could figure it out.*

Patricia often said to Angela not to be concerned, "... And live your own life. I will take care of mine."

Angela imagined—*"The Imperial Spa," no, no...that sounds too shabby. What was the name of that village with its palm-tree-lined beach I passed through? Yes, I remember, San Agustin. There it is—the "Spa at San Agustin." The spa will not be too far from the busy capital with all its tourists and be on the main highway down to this most "lus-ci-ous" beach.* Angela drew out the thought-word, as an attractive young man tiptoed gingerly on the sand exaggerating the heat of the beach no doubt to get Angela's attention. He did.

Angela was certain. She smiled, followed the handsome swimmer with her eyes down the beach, and absorbed all the tranquilly this place represented for that moment by the seagulls outlined against the azure sky. It was definitely *time for a change.* The words were bold in her mindset.

And it may free me from Hans' grip.

Chapter 8
The Goal of Homicide Detectives.

9:00 a.m. Tuesday, August 19, 2002, Bronx, New York.

The heat wave had broken as the temperature dipped to a pleasant seventy-five degrees with rain expected later in the day. Joe and Hal headed out to the Rikers Island Detention Center in their unmarked black Ford Crown Victoria police interceptor to interview the suspect in the rape/murder case.

"They actually cleaned the car for us, Hal." Joe pulled onto the Deegan for the short drive to Rikers.

"Miracles do happen." Hal tested the dash for grime and dust. "Didn't do much inside!" Hal held up a dirty forefinger and index finger for Joe to notice.

"Disgusting," Joe agreed mentally, denying the internal state of his own automobile.

Joe and Hal were sticklers for procedure and details, essential for solving homicides. Pride in the police interceptor and its appearance was an extension of their eye for exactness. At the same time, they knew their job required adaptability and flexibility—so much for the condition of the police interceptor.

Thoughts were soon on the matters before them, solving a homicide and bringing closure for the family of the victim, the overarching goal of homicide detectives.

Joe was the principal investigator while Hal handled procedural matters such as Miranda and kept notes during an interrogation or investigation. Hal may have taken some joy in cursing forensics for getting all the glory, but he truly knew the work of the homicide detectives ultimately led to apprehension of the perpetrator. This was their case and they had to solve it.

The subject of their interview was Hank Simmons, an African-American held at Rikers for an alleged involvement in a series of robberies. Trace evidence found on the victim's clothing matched Simmons' blood type. Simmons lived in the Bronx, not far from the attack on the young Latino girl. The blood match was solid evidence but Joe and Hal knew from experience that the interview was crucial. There still were loose ends.

"No one put this guy at the scene, Hal."

"I don't think it's that much of a problem. The problem was Hanratty and Jacobs fucking up the crime scene," remarked Hal.

Hanratty and Jacobs were the uniformed officers who were called to the murder site, a steep and graffiti-splattered stairway of seventy-five steps leading up to Davidson Avenue from the elevated subway entrance on Jerome

Avenue and 176th Street. Below the steps was a decayed pedestrian promenade with a couple of still-active stores.

This Bronx neighborhood had gone downhill rapidly in the last five years. Burned-out buildings, empty lots, and roaming dogs made for a scary venue famously depicted by the 1970s movie *Wolfen*. It was frightening, especially at twilight and after nightfall.

"Who knows if the first person who stumbled on the corpse wasn't the first to see the girl's body? When we arrived, the area had already been tampered with, you remember," commented Joe.

"Hanratty and Jacobs screwed up. They didn't seal off a big enough secondary area. There probably was more trace evidence that got mussed up; that's my conclusion."

Joe's annoyance showed…

"Hal, the canvass of the neighborhood didn't turn up anything either, so I don't think anything was overlooked."

Joe pulled off the exit onto the secondary roads. Rikers was in sight.

"You have everything ready for the interrogation?" Joe still sounded irritated.

Hal ignored Joe's tone. "Yep, got the Miranda card and my notebook. Does this guy have an alibi, Joe?"

"Nope, doesn't appear so. The chief says he's our guy unless he robbed the girl after she was murdered. We have to get him talking and get a confession."

Simmons turned out to be very talkative. He gave an "official statement," a confession, after twenty minutes of trying to deny any involvement, no attorney, he had waived his rights, signed the Miranda card, and was shuffled back to his cell to await trial.

Joe and Hal noticed it was almost lunchtime. They found a Subway on the way back. Joe had his usual tuna while Hal the Italian. Joe was soon humming a tune from another of his favorite musicals *Anything Goes*. He sang softly but energetically enough for Hal to hear—"It's delightful, it's delicious, it's delovely," addressing the sandwich before his next bite.

"Please not over a sandwich," pleaded Hal.

"That's me, Blimp; I often hear tunes, and they come out!"

"Well, sometimes, I think you need to keep the music to yourself."

They were both hoping to get off early. It was not to be. A fourteen-hour day lay ahead…and another new murder investigation!

Chapter 9
Enough Small Talk

As the flight proceeded from Paris to Newark, clouds formed a solid canopy over the Atlantic Ocean. Angela had convinced herself that Barbara was a person to be trusted. She believed she needed to ease into the question about U.S. Customs. It had been a half hour after dinner.

Angela restarted the conversation with Barbara.

Leaning over in the direction of Barbara, she said, "So your cruise began in Barcelona? Isn't it a wonderful city? The Gaudi architecture, for example."

Angela's broad smile and bright eyes added luster to her natural beauty.

"Oh, yes. It is a wonderful city. And you know, the oddest thing happened in Barcelona just before we arrived. They told us that the city had a hailstorm, in August, mind you, and that the people were shoveling the hail off the sidewalks! But it was all gone; just a few puddles here and there were all that was left."

"Yes, that can happen. It's the clashing of the inland colder air with the breezes off the Mediterranean. That doesn't happen in the Canaries. But to be completely candid, sometimes we get the effect of dust storms from the Sahara Desert even though the Sahara is hundreds of miles away."

"That is interesting...and where is your spa again?"

"It is between Las Palmas, you remember, the capital, and a beach called Maspalomas. Many interesting sights around there, too."

"Such as?"

"Well, there's the Cathedral de Santa Ana in the Gothic-Catalonian style, begun only a few years after Columbus discovered the New World, and many homes in the typical Canarian style—stucco with large balconies. You will see spectacular manorial houses of Latin-American colonial style. There is a museum of contemporary art and oh, the 'House of Columbus' where he stopped on his way to discovering the New World, Doramus Park, too, with beautiful gardens and flowers and a place for local folk performances throughout the year."

"We have a very beautiful spot in the United States, in Pennsylvania, that has some of the most beautiful gardens I have ever seen. Cliff, what's the name of that place, we've been there twice, with all the flowers—in Pennsylvania?"

"You mean Longwood Gardens?" Cliff leaned forward and looked at Angela.

"Longwood Gardens is also famous for its topiary," continued Cliff.

"That's it, Longwood. Are you only going to the Bronx?" asked Barbara.

"Oh no, I will send my luggage on to a Manhattan hotel. After I visit my relatives for a few days, I will tour some famous spots in the city. I do plan to stay till the end of September, so maybe I may even get to Longwood."

"Well good. It probably can't compare to your home but it is nice," said Barbara.

Enough small talk. It's time to ask. I don't want the husband involved. Cliff was still leaning forward in his seat, following the conversation. Angela's nervous uneasiness had to be satisfied.

"Barbara, I need to ask you something." Angela sank deeper back into the airline seat. Cliff took this as a signal that he should get back to reading the *New York Times* he had purchased at the terminal. *Woman talk!*

To Barbara's surprise, Angela unbuttoned the top three buttons of her dress. *My god...is something wrong? What's she going to show me?* Astonishingly, Angela was pulling out from her bra money—paper currency. Barbara recognized the Euros from recent experiences.

"I have almost $15,000 dollars here."

Barbara's jaw dropped her mouth wide open. Instinctively, she turned sideways to her left and moved forward in her seat shielding Angela from Cliff and any traffic that could pass by on the aisle. Barbara took a furtive glance over her seat at the passengers seated in row 33. *Did they hear that? Apparently not.* The woman was dosing and the man was reading one of those typical airline magazines.

"Why are you hiding that money?" Barbara whispered beginning to think she was a character in one of those classic black and white mystery/detective movies.

"I don't know what to do. The money is for my relatives. Do you think I should declare this with customs or try to get into America by concealing it? I had no problems with French customs. But I am worried that your customs will be very strict, you know, with terrorism and all."

"I have no clue. They are tightening up. But everyone probably tries to bring in something. We have some Italian leather worth about $800.00. We took the tags off and packed it in our regular luggage. But money? I don't know the rules. Is it alright if I ask Cliff?"

Angela became nervous. *What does Cliff do, maybe he's in law enforcement?*

Barbara saw the anxious smile cross Angela's face.

"It's ok. If he doesn't know, our travel companions might. They have traveled more than us."

Angela's trepidation became deeper at the thought of involving even more people in the dialogue. Angela recalled her sister's suggestion to wire the money—more than a suggestion, actually a heated exchange she and her sister had about Angela's whole idea of concealing money on her person. Her failure to consider her sister's judgment and take the advice, she now regrettably admitted, was a sign of her stubbornness. *What have I gotten myself into? I have no choice. I need an informed opinion!*

The hidden money was no longer a secret. She did not feel wonderful about that. *These are strangers. I'll never see them again, a quick goodbye when we land and no one will be the wiser.*

"Sure." Angela tried to mask her anxiety.

"Cliff, Angela has money on her. Does she have to declare it at customs?"

The question bewildered Cliff. His eyebrows rose and his face lengthened.

"Money? Why does she have to worry about money at customs?"

"Because it's a lot of money...$15,000 about...it's in Euros now but I guess that's how much it's worth."

Cliff's shrug indicated he had no clue about the rules.

"How about we ask Arty or Ben, they may know, what do you think?"

"Sure. Is that ok with Angela?"

"Yes, go ahead and ask." Barbara did not wait for Angela to respond.

Angela turned absently toward the porthole window. She realized the cascade had begun.

Cliff saw the added advantage of stretching his cramping legs. He stood and began to negotiate the narrow aisle back to the seats where Ben, Arty, and Trixie sat.

"Hi, how's everything back here?" Cliff asked Art giving a side look to Ben who glanced over from his window seat but continued reading *Art and Antiques* magazine.

"Getting some ideas for your next show, Ben?" Ben was an international dealer in nautical antiques.

Ben nodded, not saying anything. Art decided to stretch also and climbed over the dosing Beatrice sitting in the aisle seat.

"I hope I don't whack that bad foot of hers," said Art as he managed the maneuver.

As the two friends stood in the narrow aisle, Cliff got right to the point.

"Art, the woman sitting next to Barbara is asking us a question about U.S. Customs. Perhaps you would know. She has a lot of money, in Euros; she is bringing the money into the States. Does she need to declare it or can she just bring it into the country?"

Cliff then whispered, "I think it's about $15,000."

Art reflected for a moment but decided to ask his friend the antiques dealer.

"I think Ben might know. He is more of an authority." From the aisle, Art turned towards Ben.

"Ben, do customs forbid or have some sort of a limit on the amount of foreign cash you can bring into the country?"

"How much?" Ben asked still with his eyes on the antiques magazine.

Art was trying to be quiet about it but since he was standing in the aisle and did not want to disturb the sleeping Beatrice by leaning over too much, he said more loudly...

"$15,000."

"$15,000! She has that kind of money on her person!" Ben was not quiet at all.

Passengers now glanced over in the direction of the three Americans discussing someone else's money: a young man about twenty-five or so in a seat in front of the college chums; a French couple obviously on their honeymoon who sat a row behind; an elderly couple opposite the aisle returning, it seemed to Cliff, from the same cruise. *They do look familiar,* thought Cliff. With the older folks, Cliff smiled embarrassingly. They nodded back. The young couple had eyes only for each other. The young man, though, on later reflection by Cliff, seemed to turn quickly back to his cocktail not wanting Cliff to notice his interest.

The young man's shoulder-length black hair registered in Cliff's mind.

"That's right," replied Cliff to Ben not caring to repeat the amount for all to hear.

"Well, if I were her, I wouldn't say anything to Customs. They will be too busy getting me to pay taxes on the few antiques I'm bringing back," said Ben sarcastically.

Ben's detachment annoyed Art. "Be serious, Ben."

"I am serious. Hide it. Take the chance."

"Great!" Art was not appreciating Ben's flippant answers.

"Let's move, I have to go to the bathroom anyway," said Art to Cliff as they began to amble down the aisle to where Cliff had left Barbara and Angela. Just past the emergency doors were the airplane's lavatories.

"I don't know if that helped very much, Cliff," said Art as they reached row 32.

Cliff slid into his seat as Arthur paused briefly to glance at Angela. Angela stared at the back of the seat in front of her, still agonizing over the whole fuss.

"Thanks, Arty," said Cliff as Art moved on to the lavatory.

The young man seated in row 41 on the aisle noticed where Cliff took a seat and where Art paused on his way to the lavatory. He soon would venture to the toilet but only as a ruse. He wanted to get a closer look at the woman in seat 32A by the window—it was part of his ultimate plan.

"Our travel companions say not to declare the money."

Cliff made it sound as if it were a no-brainer.

Angela acknowledged only with a nod.

Chapter 10
The Spa

Patricia thought about her sister, Angela. She glanced at her wristwatch; *she is about halfway to America.*

Patricia supervised the spa staff, handled reservations and the finances for the spa. Patricia made good use of her background in banking, both the financial and customer satisfaction responsibilities she had learned in her years working at Deutches Bank in Stuttgart. Her husband, Erik, had experience in security with the same employer. He thus took care of those matters as well as the spa's buildings and grounds. Patricia was hard working. Erik lived up to Angela's too gentle characterization of "work avoider."

Erik Ruegar was a body builder type at six feet two, 210 pounds with light brown hair and blue eyes. Erik often frequented health clubs both in the old days back in Stuttgart and now in the Canaries. He obsessed over fitness. Tuesday's garb for Erik was much like any other day. He chose jeans, sneakers, and a green pocket tee. He saw in Patricia, as his gym friends would say, a "reasonably good-looking woman with a good, not great, body," a woman, nevertheless, who worked hard, reducing Erik's need to work up a sweat except on the treadmill, cycle, or power-training apparatus.

Erik Ruegar was born in Stuttgart. His parents were shopkeepers. His relationship with Patricia developed over several years since he was seventeen and Patricia twenty-two. Patricia frequented his parent's butcher shop, Papa Leon craving the homemade bratwurst that was the staple of the shop. Leon Aquino, at times, came to the shop and knowing of Erik's interest in his daughter, came to dislike the relationship. Erik hated the business since his father, who also saw him as lazy and shiftless, gave him the job of delivery boy. An opportunist if nothing else, Erik managed to skim off some money from the shop over several years. Leon Aquino worried about Ruegar's lavish spending, suspecting dishonesty. Erik disliked Papa Leon. Papa Leon did not trust Erik Ruegar.

"Erik, how are things going today." Miguel Vargas was the operator of the fitness center in Las Palmas.

"Can't complain; the spa is doing well."

Erik glanced around the facility. "Where's Bridget today; she's usually here on Tuesday mornings?"

"She called and said she won't be in today, think she is still recovering from the pulled hammy," replied Miguel, a short but muscular Spaniard who operated the center. Miguel resisted saying any more knowing of Erik's lust for Bridget, the German-born, blonde-haired, and shapely proprietor of a local health store just a few yards from the fitness facility and up the pedestrian promenade of shops and residences called Calle Mayor de Triana in the old section of Las Palmas.

"Too bad, she is a sight for sore eyes in that workout suit." Erik was never embarrassed at insinuating what it would be like to get her in bed.

"What's it going to be today?" Miguel moved from behind the counter and strutted over in the direction of the workout equipment. "Cycles, free weights, or this new upright stepper...?" he asked, his voice rising in pitch with each item of equipment. Miguel did not much like the fitness center used for liaisons. He reluctantly admitted it came with the business. Moreover, he did not like being a messenger boy either, not taking kindly to Erik's next request as Erik began on the bench press.

"Mickey." Miguel cringed at the misuse of his name.

"Mickey," repeated Erik, "I'm expecting a call sometime in the next day or two. The guy will leave you a number to call. Let me know." He paused for a second to check the weights. "And don't call me at the spa...I'll check here in person every morning and afternoon until I receive your message. Ah...let's start with 200 pounds."

With no hint of gratitude from Erik, Miguel gave an annoyed "Yeah, ok."

"Give me a fucking break, Mickey, I could go somewhere else, you know; I don't exactly see fifty million people in this place. So just do it!"

"Bridget…then you won't see Bridget." Miguel's weak retort exemplified his annoyance with the liaison scene.

"Shit. The broads are a dime a dozen. I can…I want…" Erik's words got lost under the strain of 200 pounds.

"Asshole," muttered Miguel.

Silence followed except for Erik's huffing and puffing under 200 then 225 pounds. Erik did his usual one hour on the machines after the bench press. Using the perspiration towel like a matador in the direction of Miguel, Erik left the club hoping to find Bridget at her shop.

As Miguel's eyes followed Erik out of the club, he thought, *I wish I did have more clients then I could say, "Fuck off, Erik boy."*

*****

At the spa, Patricia was checking up on the work of several housekeepers. Patricia usually dressed simply, today in a green with yellow speckled and belted cotton dress and comfortable shoes. Her black hair was tied back in a bun and she wore little make-up. Guests would be arriving in about an hour, enough time to spruce up as necessary.

Patricia was now forty-three. The years of toil at the spa had brought on early signs of age—lines on the forehead, thinning black hair, and a few extra pounds. Nevertheless, she was still an incredibly hard worker, never regretting the day Angela made the suggestion about the spa back in 1990. She accepted it—*Angela is indeed the visionary of the family. She is like Papa, both dreamers.*

Leon Aquino left a comfortable inheritance for his two daughters. Becker also had been good to both Angela and Patricia, taking a fondness to the entire family almost from the first day of Papa's work at Porsche AG. Patricia certainly suspected of the affair between Angela and Hans. She maintained a head-in-the-sand attitude, not wanting to "rock the boat." Papa and Mama would not have wanted to know if Angela's affair had anything to do with Papa's continued employment. It did not, but Patricia was never certain.

Patricia loved Angela, admitting some jealousy, however. Patricia saw herself as less capable and less attractive. She compensated by priding herself on her work ethic. She did not hesitate to clean items, even areas, if she felt the cleaning staff had neglected it. Like her mother, Patricia was slow to criticize and trusted almost everyone implicitly, the roots of her self-assurance.

The spa was popular. Angela's natural marketing ability brought the tourists as well as a good number of locals. Hans Becker always promoted the spa through word of mouth back in Stuttgart, resulting in the facility being frequented by Porsche executives as well as executives of other Stuttgart companies such as Daimler, Bosch, and Hewitt Packard to name a few. The Canaries had great golf courses with the best being Maspalomas' Campo de

Golf. Hans, who came to the Canaries as often as possible, spotted at four over par.

At the moment, Patricia was sitting at the spa's office desk a few feet behind the reception counter, unable to see any guests arriving.

"Guten Tag."

There he was, larger than life—Hans Becker had arrived at the spa in a surprise visit. He tested Patricia's German.

"Was?" Patricia answered almost automatically in German not having yet seen the face behind the voice.

"Wie geht es ihnen?" said Hans. (How are you?)

"Hans, *schauen Sie sehr kuhl.*" Patricia moved to the counter, recognized Hans, and complimented him on his "cool" look in shorts and an open shirt.

"Patricia, *das Sie schon schauen!*" (Patricia you look beautiful.)

Realizing she had no makeup on and her appearance was less than flattering, Patricia blushed pink.

"*Siezu sehen ist wie ein Schraubbolzen aus Himmel heraus.*" (Seeing you is like a bolt out of the sky).

Patricia now in English…"Ok, I still know my German; do you know your English?"

"I thought I would take few days holiday und visit my favorite folks, my favorite people!" replied Hans in halting English and with a heavy German accent.

The six-foot-two and broad-shouldered Hans threw open his big arms ready to embrace Patricia. He was dressed comfortably in red walking shorts, a flowered shirt open to the waist advertising his hairy chest, and white loafers with no socks. The sun blockers pushed over his broad forehead exaggerated his ruddy complexion stamped with a strong nose and firm mouth. His hair was colored light brown with gray temples.

"Hans, it's wonderful to see you." Patricia moved from behind the counter self-consciously brushing her dress of dust certain any particles stood out like giant boulders. The solidly built Hans warmly embraced Patricia as she planted a soft kiss on Hans' right cheek.

"Oh's wunderful to see you again," said Hans.

Becker was now sixty still with good looks, warmth, and charm that made him an attractive man. Patricia guessed that his relationship with Angela had broken up some time ago, around the time of Angela's last visit to Stuttgart in 1995. Much to his wife's anger and growing suspicions, Hans had wined and dined Angela then and introduced her as a friend and co-owner of a spa on the Canary Islands. The introductions led to many executive friends of Becker signing up for the spa for their winter sojourns. Hans hadn't been to the spa since January 2001. The distance between Angela and Hans at that time told Patricia the affair was over.

"Angela's on holiday, Hans. Left yesterday for New York." Patricia moved back slightly from Hans' continuing embrace realizing only afterwards that Angela didn't want anyone to know.

"I see, I see, vell dat's ok. Is she expected back soon?"

"No, Hans, not till the end of September."

"Oh vel, what a shame, what a shame," Hans had the habit of saying everything twice.

Patricia stepped back from Hans, addressing the reception area of the spa.

"I hope you will still find everything to your liking. Did you come alone?" Patricia was thinking of the estranged wife Angela had mentioned in the past. *Could Hans be looking to rekindle the relationship with Angela? Maybe he is escaping his wife's fury.*

"Yes, alone, alone. Everything is beautiful, Patricia." Hans was referring to the spa but his big blue eyes fixed on Patricia. Patricia's brown eyes momentarily engaged Hans. Patricia inwardly admitted to affection for Hans. Hans felt the awkwardness of the moment and so whirled around almost 180 degrees, taking in the crisp atmosphere and clean surroundings of the spa.

"But I can play golf und relax in your hot baths. Don't you be concerned, I vill be fine." Hans raised his arms seeming to take the whole reception area into his big embrace.

Hans indicated his return flight would be in five days, on the twenty-sixth of August. "Enough time to unwind und enjoy." He spoke softy, seductively to Patricia knowing of this sister's affection for him. Patricia thought that perhaps Hans sensed some of her jealousy over her sister's intimate relationship with Hans.

"Hans, I'm sorry but Angela didn't want anyone to know of her destination. She is surprising some old relatives of ours and taking in the sights."

"Ok, ok, I understand, I understand. I will keep it to myself. She felt New York vas safe these days, Patricia?"

"I know, but you know Angela, she is a very determined woman."

"Yes, indeed."

Hans then asked about local hotels. He hadn't made any reservations. Patricia indicated she would call the sophisticated and luxurious Hotel Gran Costa Meloneras about three miles away on Maspalomas Beach.

With the reservations confirmed and a taxi called, Hans took a ten-minute stroll around the grounds. Hans reentered the reception area.

"Grounds are looking splendid. Erik is still doing the work?"

Patricia hesitated, checking if anyone was in earshot. "Yes, pretty much." Then, slipping into German as a housekeeper strolled by, she said sarcastically, *"Manchmal kaum, mit Schwierigkeit."* (Sometimes barely, with difficulty).

Hans, like Angela, did not see much in Erik. He was surprised, however, with Patricia's bluntness.

"Is everything alright, Patricia?"

Patricia, realizing candor can tip off intimate details, changed the tone of her voice.

"We have some locals help with the heavier work, trees and bushes, you know, and I tend to the flowers."

Hans again complimented the spa's appearance as the cab pulled up to the spa's entrance.

"I'm off to Maspalomas. Expect me around 10:00 in the morning," shouted Hans as he dashed off to the horn-blowing cabby.

Patricia pondered how she would deal with Erik. Erik had an intense dislike for Becker. It seemed he didn't get along too well with father-figure types. He had complained bitterly to Patricia on how the auto executive doted on Angela. Erik had said there never seemed to be anything in the Becker/Aquino relationship that benefited him. The attitude hurt Patricia. She felt Erik conveniently ignored Becker's generosity to the Aquino family.

Erik's oft-repeated comment to his gym friends was, "He can shove his money and that whole company up his ass!"

Chapter 11
Long Black Hair

The Boeing 777-200 prepared for the landing at Newark Liberty International Airport. It was ten minutes behind schedule. Touch down would be at 3:40 p.m. Eastern Time.

Barbara turned to Angela. "So you don't have anyone meeting you at the airport?"

"That's right. After checking on the luggage and having it sent to the hotel, I plan to go to the Bronx and visit my relatives."

"But if they don't expect you, what will you do if no one is there?"

"You know, I haven't given that any thought; I've been so focused on surprising them." Angela revealed no hint of concern.

"Well, I do hope it works out." Barbara spoke as the overhead lights flashed, silently announcing that seatbelts needed fastening.

The landing and disembarking went smoothly enough but the luggage claim became a colossal problem. DeGualle Airport not only lacked charm. It also had the reputation for often losing luggage—tons of it!

About thirty-five passengers including Angela and the cruise group were missing luggage. The entire luggage, nine pieces for a family of six from Pennsylvania, was not on the plane. Angela's two pieces were unaccounted for as was half the luggage of Barbara and Cliff, Ben and Arthur. Only Beatrice's luggage went unscathed.

"Shit, I have those nautical antiques I purchased in Majorca in that suitcase," complained Ben.

"The photos from the trip and the Italian leather!" cried Barbara to Cliff.

"I think that suitcase held my soiled clothes," said Art laughing off the inconvenience.

But they also worried. Customs pried open all such luggage for security reasons.

"This is truly a royal pain in the ass." Cliff summed up everyone's frustration.

The delay at the airport now became intolerable. It soon was apparent that the entire luggage lost was due to transfers: Angela from Barcelona; Barbara and Cliff, Ben and Art from Rome; the Pennsylvania family and others from the cruise with the Rome connection.

"What a mess. Never again will I do this connecting-flight business." Ben had not been especially happy with other aspects of the cruise. This was the "last straw" as far as he was concerned for this travel agent. The others were less critical. The lost luggage was not the travel agent's fault, said Art.

Trixie took off in a cab for her Manhattan apartment. Art was on the cell phone telling the hired livery van to keep circling until an answer was forthcoming on the luggage. The van would take Art, Ben, Barbara, and Cliff to locations in New Jersey. It was now close to 5:45 p.m. It had been almost a two-hour delay thus far.

Angela decided she was not going to wait. She would get over to the city and hope the luggage would show up at the hotel indicated on the luggage tags.

Barbara spotted Angela. "So your luggage is lost, too?" Then Barbara realized in all the confusion, "What about customs? Angela, is everything all right, you know…?" not wanting to come out and say exactly what she meant.

"Yes, I made it." Angela spoke in a whisper while gently patting her chest. "The cigars I brought for uncle turned out to be the only concern of the agents."

Barbara smiled. "I hope this situation works out, too."

Cliff's train of thought ended as word buzzed through the waiting passengers. Air France claimed missing luggage would be delivered to everyone's address as soon as possible after it was located. Relief but also words of anger resonated through the crowd.

Angela and Barbara looked at each other and shrugged their shoulders.

"Well, goodbye and take care of yourself," said Barbara. Cliff nodded as the cruise foursome went off to the waiting van.

"What a nice person," said Barbara sweetly to Cliff.

Angela reassured herself that she had her purse, money, and carryon with the family photos and cigars for Uncle Jose. She began to make her way to the exit and taxi depot. She could tell from the arrivals slobbering through the entrances that it had begun to rain.

The terminal clock read 6:12 p.m.

As Cliff and Barbara walked away, Cliff recognized the young man from the plane standing alone some twenty yards away. *That's the guy in the seat in front of Ben, Arty, and Beatrice, the guy with the cocktail, the guy with the long black hair.*

Cliff said nothing but noticed the young man had one small piece of luggage—*apparently, his didn't get lost*—but hadn't left the terminal and seemed to be waiting for perhaps another passenger. *Traveling alone*...Cliff surmised from the seating on the plane and recall of the other passengers in that area.

The young man picked up his one piece of luggage and began to exit the terminal.

Chapter 12
"Possible Homicide!"

Overcast with showers predicted by 6 p.m. for New York City: What had started out as a clear Tuesday, August 19 was now becoming a gloomy late afternoon.

Joe and Hal had arrived back at the station at about 3 p.m. Chief Brennan had left instructions pinned crudely to the wooden frame around the glazed glass door of the office: "Complete all the paperwork on Simmons; I want a full report with closure today. Back at 6:30 p.m. Meeting downtown."

There would be no early departure for home as Joe had hoped. Joe took it all in stride. Hal did not.

"Are we expected to wait until he's goddamn good and ready? Meeting, my ass, he's probably got some honey lined up for a soirée."

Hal definitely believed Brennan was a jerk and a politico more than a dedicated cop.

"Hey, let's not think so harshly about the man. He's the boss, maybe he does take advantage of us and is inconsiderate of our time, but there's nothing we can do about it." Joe was stoic more often that not.

"And we <u>shouldn't</u> be speculating about the chief's sex life." Joe walked over to his desk, sat down, and with determination written on his face, began the task.

Hal, sounding like a medieval beadle calling the monks to dinner, decreed, "Since we're going to have to be here, what's your preference for supper? It...tal..yen, Chiii..nese, speee..cie-spiii..cie Kooo..ree...an, Koh...sher?"

"Please...shut...up!" Joe barely subdued an expletive.

They decided on Italian. (Subway does not deliver!)

*****

After finalizing the report, Joe MacLean and Hal Sweeney both burped generously from the baked manicotti and garlic bread. Chief Brennan was pleased with the paperwork. It was, however, 7:30 p.m. Joe and Hal were tired. They were hoping to clean up the office and go home.

The phone rang. Joe answered. "Possible homicide! Precede immediately to 176th Street and Jerome Ave…near the subway entrance…promenade and stairway leading to Davidson Avenue."

"Christ, Hal. It's Hanratty and Jacobs. They are securing the area. Jesus, it's almost the same spot. We have to move now!"

The site, 176th and Jerome Avenue, was one of three multi-level and high stairways leading from the elevated train platforms on Jerome Avenue with another at 173rd and Mount Eden and the third at 175th and Jerome. All three were graffiti-infested and dangerous, particularly at night.

Only 176th Street and Jerome had a 125-foot-long walkway or promenade from the street to the stairway. Three small stores bordered the promenade on the left: the Jerome Deli, a beauty salon, and a barbershop. Four stores on the right had long been boarded up, metal doors dented from vandal sticks and rocks. Three trees, barrel planters holding the precious little soil in this otherwise brick-paved esplanade and dividing the area into a left and right side, struggled to reach up for their bit of sunshine. Litter was everywhere.

Hal said nothing. Instinctively, he knew Joe was referring to a murder, a murder in the same area where the Latino girl was raped and murdered some months ago, the murder Simmons confessed to.

Blimp Sweeney latched onto the portable homicide kit, a kind of cops' tool chest with everything from paper and pencils to chalk, evidence tags, cotton as well as surgical gloves, magnifying glass, tweezers, fingerprint kit, and tens upon tens of additional items. Blimp grabbed the instamatic camera and flipped it gently over to Joe.

It was 7:38 p.m. Joe made a mental note of the time. He would later record the time in his log as "time of call." Exact location would soon be the second entry.

It was about fourteen blocks from BXTF. The police interceptor sped up the hill on the way to the murder scene.

Several police cars were already at the Jerome Avenue site. Red and blue lights flashed and reflected off the elevated subway above and the dingy shops and stores, an odd mingling of auto repairs, food stores, and a "custom window treatments" outlet. Perhaps ten to twelve uniformed cops were at the scene.

Yellow tape cordoned off the crime scene area. Not a difficult task since the promenade pitched off the main street at a perfect right angle, the yellow tape in an almost a straight line from the deli on the left to the abandoned shoe repair on the right. At the top of the high stairway, yellow tape warned people to keep out.

A light drizzle kept down the size of the curious crowd. Joe figured there were about twenty-five to thirty locals. Hal had made the call to Zone 3 homicide detective supervisor Ronald Jeffries. Jeffries said he would get there within the hour.

"The case, as usual, is yours, guys," said Jeffries.

With the portable magnetic red police beacon light flashing over the driver's side door, Joe and Hal darted from the Crown Victoria now looking like a giant black whale dripping wet.

"God help us, Hanratty and Jacobs again. Let's hope this doesn't take years to solve," mumbled Hal as they found a clear path made ready by the uniformed cops and through the onlookers to the crime scene.

Joe and Hal entered the promenade of bricked sidewalk and patches of weeds darting up among the cracks. With the El station casting its noisy, grimy presence, Joe and Hal halted at the foot of the first of five flights of stairs leading from Jerome Avenue. Joe and Hal in tandem first looked up the seventy-five steps to the top and Davidson Avenue. Then Joe and his partner looked down at the pavement. They stood and gazed at the body of a young woman lying face up at the base of those five flights of stairs, her red blood mixing with the light drizzle and blending almost artistically with the brick pavers under her body.

"What have we got?" asked Joe of Officer Bill Hanratty as he slipped on cotton gloves.

My god, thought Joe, *this is almost exactly where we came upon the Latino girl eight months ago—a rude promenade to be sure.*

Joe heard a melody in his mind. *Is it from one of those favorite Broadway shows? Did I hear it on the radio or TV? Why am I thinking of music at a time like this? Maybe it's a damn boom box in the crowd that I'm hearing.*

Recalling Hal's pleas about Joe's singing and to "keep it to yourself," Joe was comforted in his lips not moving.

But he did hear a tune, *"Rude Promenade"—no way, that can't be a song anyway! Songs are supposed to be comforting, at least the ones I hear in my head. Maybe it's something I read once, a poem perhaps by Sandburg? More like Poe! Yes, there is some poetry, call it oxymoron. Rude doesn't fit with promenade or esplanade. No...more likely a mystery story.*

The time seemed an eternity. Joe was in slow motion. He knew he had to snap out of it, no time for confusion, hesitation, mind loitering. Joe again looked to his left up the seventy-five steps. There, on the first landing up from the promenade, he saw again the Latino rape victim, her body twisted in death, lying face down on the brick landing, the steps above her bordered on each side with filthy graffiti; every four-letter dirty word possible, maybe some new ones, too, words and designs in every color imaginable— greens, blues, lots of reds, orange, white, black...

An "Are you all right, Joe?" from his partner brought him back.

Joe gathered himself. In a quiet, subdued tone, he said, "Take notes, Hal," as he stooped over the victim.

Then Hanratty spoke…

"We checked, Detective. Body is still warm, only mild rigor mortis, must have expired maybe half hour. Multiple stab wounds, possible sexual assault. Medical examiner's office is on the way."

Joe searched for identification.

"Hal make note—possible robbery. No sign of purse or wallet. Not sure of sexual motive. Breast is exposed. Bra cut from the victim. No evidence at this point of sexual penetration. Lower clothing mussed but no signs of it."

All the words Joe spoke in a kind of mechanical daze as if he was getting sick of this kind of work. Then with more enthusiasm…

"Any witnesses? Who made the call?" Joe looked over to the second officer, Harry Jacobs, who now squatted next to Joe and who had joined the three after supervising the securing of the secondary crime scene area.

"A woman walking back from the deli over there." Jacobs pointed to the corner deli, the Jerome Deli, on the left side of the promenade. "On her way up the stairs…" Jacobs moved his pointing figure to the stairs as if he was drawing an invisible line through the air.

Jacobs continued, "We have a statement, a Mrs. Gwen Owens, African-American lives up on Davidson. Saw some kids running from the scene. Kids no more than eight to ten years old."

"Doubtful perpetrators." Joe spoke as he stood up and arched his tired and aching back hoping to find relief from the fatigue.

"Get me the address of this Owens woman. Hal and I will interview her in the morning."

Jacobs nodded.

Speaking to the squatting Jacobs and looking at the victim, Joe continued, "Perhaps the kids took the purse. But no…this looks like a single perpetrator overtook this woman. She never knew what hit her. From the blood on the stairs…here…above the victim, two or three knife plunges probably into the aorta. Looks like she was heading up the stairs…perhaps perpetrator coming down. Check for any signs of blood, footprints, weapon down the walkway, up the stairs, too, never know. Look over there in that backyard, lots of grass and weeds. Knife may have been tossed over the fence."

Joe was looking intensely to his left at the green slope behind one of the apartment buildings that faced on Davidson Avenue. The hill was a visual respite from the brick, cement, and graffiti of the promenade and stairway.

Joe did not appreciate or, for that matter, even notice, the "artwork."

Jacobs stood.

"Yes, Detective," replied Jacobs, "forensics due any minute. We will instruct them also."

Jacobs left the immediate area.

"Possible robbery, I agree, but why the cut dress and sliced bra?" Joe was looking at Hal and Hanratty as all three huddled near the victim.

"You never know what these fuckers are up to, anything goes, what the hell. If he had the time, he probably thought he'd have a look," said Hal as Joe tacitly agreed while Hanratty nodded in silence.

Joe was in another funk. Music was again in his head. *Please, this is not the place!* Joe struggled to overcome his fatigue and the growing queasiness in his stomach.

"Hal, forensics must take a close look here." Joe continued, "Well, I'm going to instamatic this before the drizzle becomes a downpour. Take notes, Hal." Joe did not realize he was repeating himself.

"Ok, ok, I'm taking notes. First, describe the victim."

Taking photos at the crime scene was the specialty of the medical examiner's office. Joe learned early, however, it was a good idea to take pictures for his own records. It helped jog the memory later at a trial when accurate and consistent testimony was important.

As Joe snapped a roll of film, he described the woman and the position of the body.

"Wearing a brown knee-length dress. Sweater is navy blue with some kind of flower print. Sweater partly over her black hair, maybe she was shielding herself from the drizzle. Age maybe mid-thirties. Appears Asian, could be Hawaiian, maybe more likely Filipino. Very pretty. Lying on her back, feet bent at knee joint. Arms spread out against the brick pavers. Breast exposed, bra cut apart."

Hanratty interjected, "Detective? The medical examiner's office has arrived."

Angela Aquino had been murdered. The police had a body, a Jane Doe. It would take several weeks to discover that it was Angela. The killer made certain there was no identification left behind, at least any possible immediate identification.

The delay was crucial to the killer's plans.

Chapter 13
Searching for Clues

The medical examiner's office removed the body. Joe and Hal arranged for a canvass of the neighborhood to begin promptly at 9:00 a.m. the next day, Wednesday August 20. Told to assist were Hanratty and Jacobs. Another team of two detectives would join in the canvass; this was normal. Afterwards, Joe and Hal planned to check with the medical examiner as to the specifics of the death. They also needed to pay a visit to forensics to see if forensics had turned up any clues.

Chief Inspector Jeffries arrived at 8:55. The body had been carefully wrapped in a white sheet to protect any evidence the killer may have left behind on the body or clothing.

Darkness enveloped the region. A fog like rolling vapors at a cemetery drifted across the neighborhood. Four spotlights on portable poles punctured the vapors and illuminated the crime scene area.

"Has the area been isolated?" asked Jeffries, a stocky African-American Kojak type who stood five feet ten and weighed 195 pounds. He put the question almost directly in Joe MacLean's face. Joe caught a whiff of Jeffries' supper, heavy garlic apparently on the menu.

Joe did not let on to the inspector's bad breath. "Yes, I'm satisfied no unauthorized individuals have entered the crime scene. We have two crews searching the area now over there in the Jerome Avenue vicinity including the El and stairs. The second crew is here on the promenade and the steps leading up to Davidson. We will also get to that grassy slope behind the apartment ASAP."

"What about the graffiti-painted areas on both sides of the stairway?" asked Jeffries.

"Blimp, here, and I will hit that in a moment." Joe spoke as Hal moved next to Joe eyeing Jeffries in his gray suit, white shirt, and red tie.

"Well, good. The whole area I want cordoned off for the next twenty-four hours. Search every inch; there is always <u>something</u> left behind," Jeffries added with emphasis.

The detective supervisor continued motioning to one of the closed small storefronts on the promenade, a faded sign that announced it once was Amalgamated Hardware.

"I suggest you and Blimp set up your command post in that empty store here to the left. Pretty close to the stairs. Good place don't you think, Mac?"

Joe glanced at the faded sign and empty store. *Why not a police van instead of that dump?*

Jeffries seemed to have read Joe's thoughts. "Can't spare any more vans for the moment."

"No problem; will do, Inspector. Do you think you can send us additional detectives from homicide? Blimp and I want to check later tomorrow with the examiner and forensics?"

Jeffries enunciated every word like Professor Higgins giving a pronunciation lesson to Eliza Doolittle.

"No…more…units…can…be…put…on…this case. I told you…this…is…yours."

Seeing Hal's smirk, Jeffries added, "I'll leave some uniformed personnel if that helps. Detectives Grogan and Smith can help with the canvass. I presume you have started that process?"

"Yes, Inspector, almost at first light in the a.m." Jeffries returned Joe's smile knowing it was a lot of bullshit.

After seeing Jeffries off, Joe and Hal began a search of the graffiti-covered poured cement that buried the once grassy green border of the stairs. Several of the stairway lights were out due to vandalism and city negligence. The portable spotlights, much to the dislike of the local residents, lit up the 200-feet-wide by some 300-feet-deep crime scene area that included the street vicinity immediately off Jerome, the promenade, and the entire stairway.

The El roared by several times over the next two and a quarter hours. An evidence technician arrived to assist the three investigation crews. They slowly broadened the search from where the victim had lain to the surrounding areas. Possible blood traces were discovered leading down the stairs to where the victim lay. The light drizzle would definitely compromise the lab work.

As the investigation crews fanned out, they collected and recorded every object. They would gather bits of broken glass, several cheap brand beer cans, matchsticks, candy wrappers, a broken pair of eyeglasses, string, yellowed newsprint, a rain-soaked paperback book entitled *Yoga for Your Health*. They also bagged a broken perfume bottle, a single un-smoked cigar still banded, a woman's high-heel blue shoe size five and a half, two black buttons, half a roll of Lifesavers, and more than a few cigarette butts and used condoms.

Joe remembered the poster on the wall at homicide detective training "school."

Anything and Everything is Evidence

Nothing turned up yet in the grassy slope. *Tomorrow maybe.*

Joe and Hal were not sure if any of this stuff would help lead to the perpetrator. They were certain that they were dog-tired. Joe looked at his watch—10:45 p.m. They made their way through the posted area around the perimeter labeled "Crime Scene: Do Not Cross." They autographed the "sign-in log," indicating who they were and the time. The black and rain-beaded Crown Victoria interceptor was a welcome sight as Joe and Hal slid into the seats. Even if the big cruiser were Jonah's whale swallowing up the tired detectives, it at least meant the end of a very long day.

Joe and Hal headed for their personal vehicles in the guarded precinct lot.

"See you tomorrow in the precinct, say 9:00 a.m. Get some coffee and…?" Joe asked Hal.

"Wow, the day shift, uh? Just what you wanted!" retorted Blimp as he routinely checked his SUV for pings and dents.

Joe called out to Hal as he reached his Jetta, "You're kidding, right? This is more like the day and night shift!"

It had been almost a fourteen-hour day. Joe was not sure he would ever see Elizabeth or the kids awake again.

Chapter 14
Money Talks

The Stratton Hotel stood on the corner of 50th and Lexington Avenue, Manhattan, New York City. Recently refurbished, the new owners had done massive advertising in an attempt to lure tourists and businesspersons.

It was 8:45 p.m., August 19. The yellow New York taxi deposited its male passenger to the attention of the Stratton Hotel's waiting door attendant.

"Welcome, sir. Can I assist you with your luggage?"

As the young man paid the taxi driver and exited the cab, he replied with a Spanish accent, "No, I just have this one piece. Thank you just the same. *Muchas gracias.*"

The young man was twenty-six, five feet ten, 175 pounds, with black shoulder-length hair and fine-looking features highlighted by a well-proportioned nose, dark eyes, bushy eyebrows and olive skin. The young man had not shaved for the past twenty-four hours. He wore blue jeans, brown boots, a denim shirt, and lightweight brown leather jacket.

The Stratton's revolving doors swallowed up several people as the young man made his way into the lobby. To the right, the hotel's restaurant opened to the lobby and opposite the reception desk. A lively bar a few more feet up was ahead on the right with several patrons toasting white wine or stirring their Dewars on the rocks with a twist. Two televisions were at the bar; CNN on one, Yankees versus Toronto on the second. A sundries area was on the left just past the reception desk, elevators beyond at the rear.

The young man approached the pretty Asian-American hotel receptionist. With full confidence and no hint of deception, he casually inquired, "Hello, has a Maria Aquino checked into the hotel yet?" (The stolen purse held the hotel information.)

"What is the nature of your inquiry, Sir?"

"Yes, of course, I must explain. You see I am a cousin. Maria asked me to meet her here. She phoned me, told me she would be delayed, lost luggage at the airport."

"I see. I will check to see if the luggage has arrived." The receptionist summoned a bellman.

Knowing the old cliché that money talks...

"She also asked me to pay for the room, she would like an upgrade please to a suite if that is possible."

"Certainly, that can be arranged."

"I have come a long way myself. From Spain as you can probably tell by my accent. Could you please put the room in my name…and possibly when the luggage arrives, send it up to the room?"

The receptionist could not take her eyes off the handsome young man. His charm and polite tone stirred a spark of romance throughout her body.

"*Muchas gracias*. Here, here are my identification papers." The young man did not wait for an affirmative to his request.

He gave his name as Juan Jose Garcia Tupelos. He gave his address as Las Palmas, Grand Canaria, Canary Islands, Spain.

The address was true, but he was no relative of Maria Angela Aquino.

He was a hired killer. He specialized in knifing his victims.

Chapter 15
With Good Traffic

A shimmer of steam from the sixteen-ounce mug of Maxwell House coffee quaffed magic as MacLean held the cup in both hands and up close to his nose. He walked from the coffeemaker over to the breakfast counter.

Tired from yesterday's almost fourteen hours, Joe was nevertheless happy to be home—happy to be looking at his lovely wife as she prepared his breakfast.

"Honey? Are you sure you're ok?" asked Elizabeth MacLean as she brought her husband a generous portion of hot oatmeal.

"I hope this doesn't turn into a day and night shift. The kids will never see you!" Liz stroked the back of Joe's head.

"Tired, that's all. New case last night. You know the routine. Blimp and I are doing the canvass this morning. See what we can find out."

"No idea who she was, uh?"

"No ID. Running photo, prints, whatever through the labs. We'll see."

"Was she wearing a wedding ring?"

"No, not from what I could tell. No ring marks."

Just then, Jenna, their eight-year-old, seemed to almost crash through the back kitchen door. Chips, the family's six-month-old Japanese Chin, trailed behind as Jenna tugged on the leash fastened to the harnessed eleven-pound white and black dog.

"Really," exclaimed Liz, "do you have to make so much noise? Cory is still sleeping!"

Jenna had quickly donned a pair of white shorts, yellow tee shirt, and yellow sandals in order to meet her responsibilities to the new pet.

Jenna just smirked knowing the next question would be her father's usual and emphatic inquiry…"**Did he do his business?**"

Chips was still not completely trained to dump or pee outdoors instead of in his two-by-three-by-four cage or, on occasion, in front of the kitchen sink which on two instances Joe had stepped into, once with bare feet. Joe and Liz knew this would not be easy since the breed had a reputation as difficult to train.

"Yes, Daddy, number one," Jenna announced triumphantly.

Joe had given Chips two, maybe three, more weeks or it was sayonara for the big-eyed, longhaired purebred dog. It was purely a lap dog, absolutely of no watchdog value. Joe did admit Chips was cute and good for the kids.

Joe checked the kitchen clock: 8:10 a.m., time for a few more spoonfuls of hot oatmeal. He enjoyed hot cereal all year round, with plenty of Aunt Jemima Syrup.

"Glad to hear it!" Joe gave Jenna a big smile. Jenna had seen Chips in a local pet shop and begged Liz for the chance to prove she could take care of her new pet. He still had to be neutered.

"Will you be late again, Daddy?" asked Jenna with a sigh.

"I think I can be home between five and six. What do you have in mind?"

"Softball game at 6:30, remember?"

"Of course, over at Federal Field, right…same as last time?" Joe gave Jenna a big hug. "I'll join Mom and Cory, no problem."

"What time are you supposed to meet Blimp?" Liz poured more coffee and then cleared the empty oatmeal dish from the table.

"Yep…it's getting late. Promised to start the canvass right after nine."

Jenna looked up as Joe and Liz embraced. Joe stroked Liz's long blonde hair and gave her a big kiss. Chips seemed to notice too as he braced his two front legs on the bottom rung of the kitchen chair and gave a yelp.

"I will call if anything comes up."

Joe grabbed his shoulder harness, checked the safety pin of his weapon, and with Liz removing the light blue cotton summer jacket from the back of a kitchen chair, he picked up Jenna saying, "Love you, kid."

Cory was sneaking a peek around the kitchen archway, his blue with white teddy bear nightshirt touching the wood floor. Cory made a dash for Joe, receiving an equally loving hug, kiss, and "Love you, too, kid!" exclamation.

Liz planted another kiss on Joe as he opened the front door. She added, "Please drive carefully. Love you!"

Joe made his way around the tricycle on the short front walk leading to the driveway to his left. The Jetta, still in need of a good cleaning in and out, stood parked next to Liz's metallic tan Pathfinder. Liz kept the SUV very clean and polished.

Joe blocked it all out. With good traffic, he would arrive at BXTF by 9:10.

Chapter 16
A Light Drizzle Moistened the Air

The upgrade to a suite at the Stratton Hotel on the 24th floor was a beginning. Garcia Tupelos was enjoying himself with the victim's money. The girl from the escort service had been exquisite. *She took Euros, too. No questions.* Questions were not useful in a prostitute's business.

Room service was fair: club sandwich of turkey and bacon. Two bottles of light beer proved very enjoyable. He had just made the room service deadline of midnight. The killer would sleep soundly, thinking of the 50,000 Euros promised for the **next** murder.

*****

Angela's murderer awoke at 7:35. He had to remember the time difference between New York and Gran Canaria. *What was it...yes...six hours, making it 1:35 p.m. on the island?* He had to place a call at 3:30 p.m. Gran Canaria time. *That makes it 9:30 in New York. Plenty of time for breakfast.* Room services once again...*the fewer people who see me in the hotel, the better. Later, change some money and after that...buy some clothes.* The Euros would convert to almost $14,000 and he had the $600.00 in USA currency Angela had in her purse. *Probably change three or four thousand, that's plenty and will keep me in style for the three days before the return flight to Barcelona. Pay cash for everything. Have to dump the purse, carryon, and suitcases! Make certain nothing could link that stuff to Aquino. Was there such a thing as a Goodwill depot in Manhattan? There's always Air France; they're certain to lose it! Ha, ha!*

Tupelos ordered breakfast from room service. He walked lazily over to his hotel room window and separated the sheer curtains, giving him a clear view of morning traffic down on Lexington Avenue. He stood admiring the view, his only threads black silk boxers. Reaching over to the desk near the window, he picked up his pack of Marlboros and a Bic lighter. He lit up the cigarette and inhaled deeply.

Garcia Tupelos recalled his stalking of Angela at the terminal.

Lucky to get a cab right behind her cab. Told the driver... "1727 Davidson Avenue. I'll double the fare if you get me there fast."

And then there would be that incredible stroke of luck when the Angela's Jersey taxi couldn't find Davidson Avenue.

The killer's taxi driver had warned him of some of the bad neighborhoods in the Bronx. Subsequent discussion led him to tell the driver to drop him off near the El at Jerome and 176th. It sounded as if there would be more people there. At least that was what he wanted the driver to think.

He remembered making his way up the stairway, a tough climb even for his athletic body. He looked down the seventy-five stairs...one of the five brick-paved landings a few feet below…black-painted and rusty pipe railings on each side of the stairway…basement support wall of an apartment building that faced onto Davidson to his left.

He pictured again the three scrawny trees dividing the promenade. He saw the El. Then, to the right, was the roof covering the three stores on the promenade. To the extreme right, there was a high fence dividing the stairway from the back property of another apartment building facing Davidson.

The stores closed. It was deserted and gloomy. A light drizzle moistened the air. He recalled how the air seemed unusually cool for an August evening.

He turned slightly to his right. He could see that it was only a few yards to 1727 on the opposite side of the street and to the left of the stairs. Number 1727 was a yellow brick building with an arched white stone double doorway painted brown. It was a symmetrical building design dating to the 1930s with five floors of twenty, one-bedroom apartments. Dual fire escapes perched over the archway leading from each kitchen window on floors two through five.

The building was in good condition but was flanked on both sides by empty lots where former apartments once stood. He saw down the street the one-story storefront, Mt. Pleasant Pentecostal Church.

Tupelos recalled how his plan needed flexibility as well as caution. For the moment, the plan called for killing Angela just inside the doorway with a hood to cover his face if necessary.

He planned for two very quick knife plunges into the chest. *Then I'll cut the bra off, get the money. Gather up her purse and carryon. Stuff the purse in my bag, big enough to hold it. Carryon could be either for a man or for a woman. No problem there.*

The early evening rain kept most folks off the street leaving fewer people to notice. The rain would wash away any blood carried onto the pavement. He hoped!

Two firm knocks on the hotel room door interrupted the killer's reflections. It was room service. He dispatched the waiter quickly, rewarding him with a five-dollar tip.

A breakfast of ham, eggs, muffins, and coffee became a pleasant respite from the grisly details of the murder.

As he sat down to enjoy his breakfast, he knew he had to review last night's details. He had to make certain he had not overlooked anything.

I was waiting at the top of the stairs. Tupelos had a good view from there to his left and down the one-way street that was Davidson Avenue. It would be easy to spot any cab coming around the corner from East 174th Street and onto Davidson and give him enough time to cross the street and enter the lobby. He turned again to glance down the stairway to Jerome. The passing El thundered by.

Then came the turn of events that he was certain in his mind would make this a perfect crime!

Shit, that was the surprise of the evening, thought Tupelos.

A cab was dropping off its passenger on Jerome, at the foot of the stairs…maybe one hundred feet or so from the first set of stairs. He remembered…*I was just down there after all. It is Angela!* He had no trouble recognizing the brown dress and the blue sweater now a cover from the drizzle. She was paying the driver; he seemed to be pointing up to the top of the stairs. She was nodding expressively. *If I hurry down the stairs, I could kill her coming up the stairs. Very quick, one or two plunges will do it, then the rest as planned. Oh, this is prefect...the train will get me out of here fast. No one around right now. But would it stay that way?*

The woman was passing the third barrel-embraced tree and approaching the first set of stairs. The killer dashed down the stairs in leaps and bounds. His satchel bounced up and down on his back.

Angela would never sense the impending danger. Patricia's lovely blue sweater covered Angela's head, protecting her from the rain. Angela had just reached the first landing, her eyes focused on the crumbling steps—not on the killer dashing down the stairs.

It was over quickly.

The first thrust in the abdomen. There was little, if any, initial blood. That was the plan! *Keep the blood at a minimum....splatter and all!* The second blow went deep into the lungs and heart.

Angela bolted straight back down the stairs from the force of the blows, landing face up at the base of the stairs, legs bent at the knees…arms spread wide on the pavement, the blue sweater remaining on most of her black hair, the rest held tightly in her right hand.

Angela's body lay the way Joe and Hal would find her.

Tupelos recalled that he now had to act quickly. He slit the dress and cut the bra in two quick cuts. *Yes, there it is…the money just as those fools on the plane had discussed and stuffed into the cups of the bra. My information was correct.* (The "fools" had mentioned the money. Instructions to strip off the bra had come from another source.)

He remembered hearing kids at the top of the stairs. Quickly, the killer stuffed the purse in the larger satchel… and grabbed the carryon. *Damn, dropped it…*

A few things spilled out. He gathered them up. *Hum, cigars, too. Enjoy one later. Ok, down this filthy alley...up the El stairs. Take the train to Manhattan. Looks good, only those damn kids...but too far away to identify.*

Then, as he headed to the subway, *Shit that fat fucking black woman with the groceries! Just brushed her rushing to the El. No matter.*

As fortune would have it, the killer caught the train almost immediately. It sped him on his way to Manhattan and the hotel.

As Tupelos sipped his morning coffee, he compared the murder of Angela to a few of his other hits.

Fuck, this was an easy one.

The kids were too far away. Mrs. Owens was not.

Chapter 17
The Canvass Begins

The canvass of the neighborhood began at 9:30 the day after the murder. The shoe leather hit the pavement or, as it turned out, the mud of the grassy slope.

Joe and Hal worked the odd-numbered apartment buildings on Davidson Avenue. Hanratty and Jacobs checked with the owners and employees of the stores on Jerome Avenue. No residences were located down on Jerome. Two additional uniformed officers searched the grassy slope. Detectives Grogan and Smith worked the even numbers on Davidson.

As directed by Inspector Jeffries, the detectives and uniformed cops had set up a command post in the defunct hardware store near the steps and on the promenade.

The day was clear and bright unlike the previous day.

The Asian residents received special attention since the victim was of Asian ancestry. No one yet was certain which ethnicity.

As the interviews proceeded, no one claimed to see anyone or anything unusual at the foot of or the top of the stairs between 6:45 and 7:15 the night before, the approximate time of the murder. No one had seen anything either the night of the rape and murder of the Latino girl. Granted, the stairway was not in many people's direct view from any apartment or shop window. A few fire escapes at the back of the apartment buildings that faced Davidson did overlook the roofs of the stores and warehouses on Jerome. However, it was not likely that someone was sitting out on a hot and rainy night.

"Still plenty of daylight," said Joe as he and Hal climbed to the third floor of 1727 Davidson, "yet no one claims to have seen anything that would help us."

Blimp was trying to catch his breath after the two flights up to the apartment of Gwen Owens, the woman who called the police after discovering the body.

Joe had sprinted up the stairs and looked back at Hal as Blimp eyed the last three stairs.

"Don't even fucking think it."

Owens lived in an apartment like all the rest at 1727 Davidson. There was a small eat-in kitchen to the left after you entered the apartment. The good-size living room held a three-cushioned sofa, two easy chairs, and an old-fashioned console TV with radio and record player done in cherry veneer. Completing the layout were a bedroom and at the rear of the apartment and just before the bedroom, a bathroom off to the left.

Owens led the detectives into the living room and asked them to have a seat on the sofa, covered with a tan throw tucked in neatly under the cushions. Owens slowly made her way to the swivel easy chair and turned it away from the TV so she faced the detectives. An oxygen tank stood next to the chair.

Joe inwardly derided Hal for his poor conditioning. *This poor woman has to struggle every day with those stairs.*

Joe began the questioning.

"Mrs. Owens, can you tell us anything more about what you saw last night before you called the police?" Joe realized his tone was overly sympathetic.

"Actually, my friend, Maureen, on the first floor called. I didn't want to wait till I got to my apartment. It'd been awhile if I had to climb those stairs to the third floor."

Hal spoke. "About how long did it take you to get to your friend's apartment from where you discovered the victim?"

"I did pretty good this time, feelin' the urgency and all. I'd say about fifteen minutes."

Joe made mental note of the delay. *Enough time for someone else to come along, maybe cut the bra, even steal a purse.*

Joe spoke firmly now. "Mrs. Owens, you said you saw a few youths run away form the scene?"

"That's right, that's what I told the policeman last night."

"But did you see anyone else in the area?"

"It was rainin' and I was comin' back from the store. I didn't see anyone else on the promenade." The excitement of the questioning was beginning to tell on Owens as she turned and reached for the oxygen.

"That poor woman. I felt so bad." Owens took a few deep breaths of oxygen.

Joe felt that the questioning had to end. "I see. Well, Mrs. Owens, if you should recall any additional facts that might help us please give the station a call."

"It's just awful. You know, that makes two murders on that promenade in the last six or seven months. I reported both of them you know." Owens struggled visibly, hesitating, nevertheless, to use the oxygen again until the detectives left.

Joe and Hal looked at one another. They both thought about the Latino girl's rape and murder. *Are we missing something here? That was not our recollection.*

Mrs. Owens had forgotten to tell the detectives of her brush with the young man with the long black hair.

After Joe and Hal made inquiries with the remainder of the residents at 1727, they moved on to 1733. No one in any of the apartments was helpful to the investigation.

As the detectives made their way to the command post on the promenade, Hal had a thought.

"Joe, you know the Owens woman could be right. We picked up that murder case from those two dickheads that got transferred to Brooklyn, those arrogant fucks that Brennan couldn't stomach."

Joe could only think of what Chief Brennan thought of Blimp with his contrary personality.

"Yep, that certainly could be."

Then Blimp had another idea, this one more on target.

"Perhaps the victim did not live in the area. We will have to check with missing persons. May be something on file! Or maybe she was visiting the area. We should have asked about relatives or friends of the folks living up there."

"Good, Blimp, if I recall 1727 and 1733 had a number of Asian families. Let's try again. Perhaps they were expecting a visitor."

Joe and Hal trekked the route once more. Hal did not grumble about the climb this time.

As it turned out, a family at 1733 was expecting a guest on Friday, but a male, not a female. At 1727, no one was expecting a visitor. Three Asian-American families lived at 1727. Joe and Hal recorded the names: Bonita, Shim,

Valencia. Bonita and Valencia were actually Filipino; Shim Vietnamese.

In was nearly 1:00 p.m. Joe and Hal were anxious to get to the forensics lab out in Jamaica, Queens for results. Hanratty, Jacobs, and the two cops assigned to the El had turned up nothing. Grogan and Smith were still working their side of Davidson. They would report to Joe later in the day. More questioning became necessary there because of the fire escapes facing the crime scene. The four uniformed cops stayed and continued to secure the area as they had done the previous night. They also interviewed anyone who approached the stairway.

Joe and Hal realized they had to be present at the autopsy in order to confirm the victim if not her identity. They changed their plans. They decided to head directly to the medical examiner's office on First Avenue, Manhattan. Forensics would come later, perhaps not until Friday.

Wednesday's weather was turning out to be exceptional with temperatures around eighty degrees. The interceptor's air conditioner made the inside a comfortable sixty-five degrees.

"Was this woman a chance victim or was she sought out by the killer?" Joe spoke as they approached the FDR Drive heading downtown.

Driving down the east side of Manhattan, they passed under the Hospital for Special Surgery, passed the turnoff to the Queens Midtown Tunnel, and came upon Bellevue Hospital. They turned off at the East 23rd Street exit and then headed up north on First Avenue to the examiner's offices.

On the passenger side, Hal positioned the visor to block the bright sunlight.

Hal commented, "We appear to have a robbery and at minimum, a molestation. That would tend to lean on the side of chance."

"Right. But, Hal, it doesn't appear that she lived in the area and nobody was expecting a visitor. Could she have been a dealer? Killed for money and drugs? The bra was sliced...Hal, it could be! Forensics may tell us if there was heroine or cocaine on the dress, on the bra, or on her breast."

"Could have been a prostitute, too. A pimp may have done her in," continued Joe, glancing out the car window to his right as the police interceptor neared their destination.

Hal reflected and then spoke. "Maybe you're right on the first thought. Drug dealers could have murdered her. If she was dirty, we should have prints on file. And if she was a whore, we'll know that, too."

Hal sounded as if a motive was in sight. His face mirrored satisfaction. Rounding up the usual suspects would lead to clues as to the victim's identity.

As for the late Angela Aquino, she was still only a Jane Doe, thought of as anything but the astute businessperson and loving sister of Patricia.

Hal picked up the conversation...

"We may have to check with immigration. She could have just arrived here and we wouldn't have anything."

Hal was being more imaginative than usual. Hal put on a smug smile. Joe looked over. Blimp was thinking prejudice—All Asians must be just off the boat. Joe recognized the expression.

After all, that, too, had become a well-practiced exchange between the partners.

Chapter 18
A Killer's Call

Tupelos changed some Euros into dollars. The bank had no problem since Tupelos had shown proper identification. He went afterwards to some high-end shops on Fifth Avenue and purchased new clothes and boots. He kept with his preferences—jeans and leather. He planned to ditch his murder garb. *And why not use Angela's luggage, two pieces, was it? Take the tags off, make good use of it, difficult to ditch anyway.* The purse was easy, just an ordinary city trash can.

Angela's luggage was delivered dutifully to Room 2429 at the Stratton Hotel. Tupelos dumped the contents on the king-size bed. *That whore last night could have fit into some of these clothes…Oh nice, very nice lace.* Tupelos held up a pink panty. *And the perfume, yes, I recognize it from the islands. It all has to go, what a shame.*

Angela's clothes would end up in city trash receptacles over the next two days.

The killer's call to Las Palmas was short. He placed it at exactly 9:30 a.m. New York time from his hotel room. To the person on the other end of the long-distance call Tupelos gave a phone number and a brief instruction.

He then quickly hung up the phone.

Chapter 19
Silver, Black, and Gray

Thursday, August 21 would have been Maria Angela Aquino's fortieth birthday. Now, she was dead, having never made it to the big four-zero. She never celebrated with the Valencia family. Instead, her body was stretched out on the autopsy table in the medical examiner's office at 520 First Avenue, New York City.

Silver, black, and gray dominated the autopsy room. The white sinks and body organ scales along with the puke-yellow tiled walls added to the sterile, cold appearance. The floor was gray tile, like the color of death. The smell of ammonia dominated.

Angela's body measured and weighed at five feet three inches and 103 pounds. It had been X-rayed as well, the fatal stab wounds in the abdomen and chest destroying an otherwise healthy and vibrant individual.

Dr. Janet Reynolds was the pathologist in charge. She was filling out the homicide worksheet and waiting for Detectives MacLean and Sweeney. They had called with their approximate time of arrival.

A medico-legal autopsy was always required in a murder investigation. The cause of death, the manner of death, and the mode of death all were the purview of the pathologist/ medical examiner.

Upon arrival of the homicide detectives, Reynolds had completed the first portion of the worksheet: the age was thirty-nine to forty-one, female found at 176th Street and Jerome Avenue, and the date of autopsy. Still to be determined was positive identification such as name and residence. Joe and Hal would contribute information as to the exact location of the body and circumstances of the death.

The morgue was never a pleasant place. It was no walk through the flowers. Hal called it the "dead house." Joe and Hal cautiously passed a few draped corpses. Reynolds, a short plump woman of forty-two, greeted them. Originally from Iowa, Janet Reynolds earned her degree from Iowa State University. She had not lost her Midwestern drawl after seven years in the Big Apple.

"Janet, how are you today? Are we ready to go?"

"It's a real shame, Joe...beautiful woman...every indication of excellent health and physical condition." As Reynolds spoke, she pulled down the white sheet uncovering Angela's body to the waist.

"Jesus, Mary, Joseph." Joe backed slightly away from the examiner's table, touched his lower lip, then squeezed it gently and continued, "Yes, that's the woman we found last night."

Hal had said nothing but was taking notes as well as reviewing his scribbles from the night before. He also held the instamatic photos Joe took at the scene. Hal looked at two or three and stopped with the front facial photo. He showed it to Joe. They both nodded in agreement.

"What can you tell us, Doctor?"

"The victim died almost instantly. The first stab wound, as you can see here, penetrated the lower left quadrant just below the diaphragm. This would cause death by bleeding but it would not be instantaneous, also not much initial flow of blood."

Reynolds placed her gloved fingers near the fatal wound.

"This penetrated the thoracic cavity, heart and lungs received much damage. A knife, I would say about five to six inches and a thick blade, was pushed in and then up, tearing the vital organs, a very powerful blow. I'd say a strong male did this."

"That would be consistent with the killer coming down the stairs, running or sprinting down the stairs perhaps, and plunging the knife with great force. Hal, make note that the wounds are consistent with our initial examination."

"There is also trauma to the upper back and rear of the head. The victim was pushed back then and fell down a flight of stairs?"

Hal read from his notes. "That's right. We found traces of blood at the landing about six to seven feet above from where the victim was found."

"That makes the head and back marks post mortem. Can you tell us if the killer was left- or right-handed?"

"No-oo doubt left-handed, Joe."

"That's a big clue. Any evidence of drugs, alcohol?"

"None. And she was not a prostitute. Internal exam shows no semen."

"So what are left are fingerprints, teeth, and maybe clothing identification."

"That stuff is being worked on out in Queens, Joe. Van Bergen was here this morning."

Dr. Reynolds was referring to the forensics experts, Joe and Hal's next stop.

"Van Bergen's good. Well, it's 4:15, Hal. Forensics will wait till tomorrow or Friday."

Hal now realized, *I guess the usual suspects will not do!*

Chapter 20
Automatic Now

The police interceptor reached the newly opened NYPD Forensics Laboratory: an entirely remodeled old department store on Jamaica Boulevard a few blocks from Jamaica Center, the area's lively shopping district. The time was Friday, August 22, 9:45 a.m. The department's Forensic Investigation and Crime Scene Division was housed here in one of the most modern forensic labs in the country. The facility held a host of specialized forensic departments including ballistics, arson, trace evidence such as hair and fiber, drug analysis, and latent prints. Computerized evidence tracking linked the facility to forensics labs throughout the country with the goal being a national network in the hunt for criminals and ultimately for convictions.

Joe signaled to turn left off Jamaica Boulevard onto the side street that led to the parking garage in back of the forensics lab. Hal noticed the Rufus King Manor Museum on the right…"It's amazing that we have this little piece of American history…greenery amidst this hubbub."

The colonial-style home dated back to the 1790's. Painted a pale yellow with black shutters, the home had a black roof with a white-columned portico entrance. Once the home of Rufus King, New York delegate to the Constitutional Convention, these days it had few visitors. Centered on an eleven-acre picturesque park, the homestead was directly opposite forensics.

"Well," said Joe self-congratulating his insight, "in many ways, it's quite a contrast to this side of the street, a twenty-first-century high-tech building."

As Joe pulled into the parking garage, "About the only thing they have in common is this pale yellow," continued

Joe referring to the yellow brick that a few years before held an Abraham and Strauss department store.

The modern facility bore no resemblance to its days when it held everything from women's lingerie to fur coats. Joe and Hal took the elevator to the third floor of the four-story building. After waiting a few minutes in an outside reception area, Joe and Hal were buzzed into the corridor that led to the offices of lead forensic trace evidence scientist Dr. Cara Van Bergen. Van Bergen was twenty-eight, very pretty with blonde hair, blue eyes, and a clean and fresh Dutch-like face and complexion.

"Well, hello, Joe, and welcome, Hal, good to see you again. Looking for clues, are you, for this promenade slaying?" Van Bergen's sonorous voice matched perfectly with her smooth look and lean figure.

Joe thought again...it was automatic now in his brain receptors...*the **rude promenade** you mean*!

"What did you say, Joe? You mumbled," asked Van Bergen as her blue eyes squinted slightly with the question.

Joe, realizing he might have uttered "rude promenade," quickly interjected, "Nothing, it's nothing. What did you discover? Something that will help?"

Hal took out his notebook, leafing to the notes taken at the murder scene.

"I think so, but in some ways, it's very strange."

Joe and Hal's ears were fully engaged.

"Strands of long black hair…human…Caucasoid… from the head with no dyes or treatments. A loose hair, not pulled, so no roots. We're not able to determine sex without the roots. Couple more tests on that…maybe turn up something."

"Victim was Asian, we think. So maybe a white guy did this in a minority area?"

Van Bergen and Blimp remained silent during Joe's rhetorical question.

"And what's so strange then?" Blimp sounded mildly critical.

"Well, first, we can say it's not the victim's hair because she treated her hair. But here's the strange part...we also found fibers on the dress, the bodice area, that look like they come from paper currency. Very strange. Long way to go yet on that one."

"Not strange if she was a prostitute or dealer, don't you think?" commented Hal incredulously.

"Hal, the examiner ruled that out, remember?"

Van Bergen's look said she agreed. She took a breath and added, "And from the stuff you gathered from the pavement...the cigar you found?"

"We remember...un-smoked and banded," replied Blimp trying to recover after his ill-advised remark about the Jane Doe being a prostitute.

"Right, it appears to be a very expensive brand...not common. We'll determine the maker and origin within a few days."

"Very interesting, not money and drugs, but money and cigars!" Blimp had to hold back a hardy chuckle or two.

"You say it's an expensive brand?" inquired Joe.

"Yes, from the purity and tight wrapping…could be Cuban. Not my area, though; I'm guessing here. Conrad, our investigator, will look into it."

"No, no, it's a good conjecture at this point. Hal, what do you think?"

"With the traffic in that area, my guess is the stogie belonged to the perpetrator. Probably wouldn't be laying there very long, too good to pass up by the locals or some street bum. Perpetrator may have dropped it."

"So maybe we have a left-handed killer who likes high-end smokes. Not much but it's a start." Joe accepted progress in small increments.

"And the clothing…" started Van Bergen.

"Yes?"

"High quality and the label indicated it was manufactured in Spain."

"Wow. This is beginning to look like a sophisticated lady murdered by a white guy with dough."

"That's it for now, Lieutenants." Van Bergen reached out to shake hands first with Blimp and then Joe.

Joe and Hal indicated they would check back in a day or two. It was off to BXTF for reflection. The detectives believed they had slowly inched forward.

They could not have realized. They were several thousand miles and an Atlantic crossing from the solution.

Chapter 21
"The One is an I..."

Patricia was still anxious as to how Hans and Erik would get along. *Maybe through some miracle, their paths will not cross.*

Friday, August 22 proved again to be a clear and bright day on Gran Canaria. Patricia planned a drive up to Las Palmas. She needed new linens for the spa, maybe some fresh flowers too for the reception area.

The temperature was eighty-two degrees at 9:15. Patricia hoped to be back by 1:30. She decided to leave a note for Hans saying she had some errands to do and could not be at the spa at his expected time of arrival, 10:00 a.m. Hans was always very prompt, never known to be late for anything. She wished, too, that Erik would see the note and make himself absent for the day.

Patricia always made herself look her best when going to town. She wore a yellow sweater, white skirt, and white sandals. Her black hair was long and straight. Lipstick was a cool pink with a little bit of blush on her cheeks. Eye makeup highlighted her brown eyes. She plucked a few stray hairs from her black eyebrows. As she examined her fingernails and toenails, she decided it was time for a manicure and pedicure. *Maybe enough time today?*

Driving on the GC1 highway linking San Agustin with Las Palmas, Patricia never tired of the magnificent scenery. The 2001 silver-with-black-leather-interior Volvo Turbo had no problems with some of the rugged and steep grades. The drive, about thirty miles, meandered along the coast close to the ocean. The ocean, after about fifteen miles out of San Agustin, splashed white and high off the red, blue, and yellow fire-like rocks along the shoreline. As the road turned toward the provincial capital, the ocean was now some 175 feet below.

Most of the population drove motorcycles, mopeds, and motorized bicycles. Nevertheless, it could happen even out here: oxen dragging a grain-laden wagon across the road. The thought prompted Patricia to reflect on many of the old customs dating back to the early part of the twentieth century. She pictured young women in wide green skirts, decorative aprons, white, loose-fitting blouses, and bright yellow or pink shawls sewing intricate patterns. She heard costumed musicians singing folk songs in one of the many esplanades. Women in wide-brimmed straw hats carried Canary pine seedlings to trucks for planting in some of the denuded areas from the old ship-building days. Although increasingly rare, these sights were still possible on the islands.

The road sign indicated Las Palmas was now one kilometer. Patricia, like her sister, was a true Canarian known for their historical hospitality. Navigators such as the Berbers, the Germanic peoples, the Nordics plundered the coasts betraying this kindness, really naiveté. Patricia was welcoming, but naïve like the early aborigines of the islands.

This naiveté would soon be borne out.

Patricia's destination, the dry goods shop, was located in the heart of the old town, on a pedestrian promenade. Patricia parked about a quarter kilometer and walked. She looked down at her open shoes pounding the cobblestones and reminded herself to stop in at the salon. *Here we are... Calle Mayor de Triana.*

While Patricia knew Erik frequented the fitness center on the promenade, she was not aware that Erik was there now inquiring of Miguel regarding any messages. Patricia did not keep a record of her husband's comings and goings. After purchasing the linens, Patricia walked back to the beauty salon.

"No problemo, dearie, we can give you the treatment in about twenty minutes," said Charles, the openly gay salon owner.

The salon was located a few shops up from Bridget's health foods store. Patricia never went to health stores, or gyms for that matter. Exercise in the spa gardens and watch what you eat were her mottos.

Inside the gym, Erik was not interested today in a workout, only if there were any messages.

"Yes, a guy called yesterday. Didn't give his name. Said to call him at this number. Here, I wrote it down for you." Miguel handed Erik a notepad-size piece of paper.

Erik looked at the number: 1-201-941-5145.

"Was that it...anything else?"

"Only that he said to tell you...'The one is an I...' whatever the hell that means?"

"Thanks, Miguel. There may be more calls. I'll stop in again."

Miguel noticed the deliberate attempt by Erik to be considerate for a change. *Must be good news,* thought Miguel.

Erik decided to visit Bridget on the Calle Mayor de Triana.

Back at the spa, Hans found Patricia's note. Hans decided on a full-body massage. Perhaps by that time, Patricia would return.

Chapter 22
Shoptalk

Friday afternoon back at BXTF, Joe and Blimp leafed through several reports. The report by the other detectives searching the grassy hill area next to the promenade and stairs proved inconclusive. No murder weapon, no additional leads as to the identification of the Jane Doe.

"I think we need to sit on this a few days, Hal." Joe wanted the day to end and the weekend to begin.

As Blimp began to move from behind his desk, he said, "Maybe on Monday, we'll see something we're overlooking now. I need to get an early start out to Selden, Joe."

"It would be nice. Chief Brennan left nothing new for us to look into. Thank god, the weekend is looking good."

Hal noticed a puddle of water under the office air conditioner.

"Joe? Shit, look at that goddamn water. No wonder it is fucking hot in here. That goddamn AC is on the fritz."

"It can wait until Monday, Blimp. Let's get the hell out of here before Brennan comes up with something for us to do."

Joe arrived home in Garnerville at 4:30. Liz and the kids were happy to have Joe for the weekend.

Joe said, "How about dinner out, honey? Can we get a sitter on this short notice?"

"I can try Katie. I think her Mom said she was staying home tonight."

"Let's go to that Tuscany restaurant over in Nyack. You call the sitter and I'll see about reservations."

Cory entered the family room. "Hey, kiddo, I'm going to get you." Joe pretended to be a Hulk-like figure. Cory screamed, knowing what was coming, his Dad chasing him around the family room until Daddy launched one of his tickle attacks.

"Katie is all set. She can come over at 6:00. I said we'd be home by 9:30."

*****

The dinner was splendid. Joe had his favorite: rack of lamb with a mustard and rosemary crust. Liz enjoyed the homemade ravioli stuffed with portabella mushrooms. The wine was a delightful and inexpensive, California chardonnay. The pushy waiter did try to push a bottle of French Merlot at $45.00 a bottle.

Liz allowed for a bit of shoptalk knowing Joe had something on his mind.

"Any leads on that Jane Doe case?"

"Well, the medical examiner and forensics have given us some leads. Still no clue as to her identity. To me, it's a mystery as to what she was doing there. No indication either of where she lived or that she was calling on someone. She was clean for drugs and prostitution. She possibly was well off, fine-tailored cloths made in Spain. Good physical condition, well-toned body. Robbery, yes…but the killer seems to have covered his tracks…made sure no purse or wallet found. Not terribly unusual, come to think of it."

"Joe, can't we go on vacation soon. You have been working without a break for too long. I want to go to Savannah, remember?" Liz sounded mildly pleading.

Liz had wanted to spend some time in Savannah ever since she had read *Midnight in the Garden of Good and Evil* some years ago.

"Liz, you know I don't particularly like to fly. Do we drive?"

"But the flight can't be that long. We would waste time driving down."

"Planes, delays, and tight security now...I don't know." Joe was shaking his head in the negative. He took another sip of his decaf.

Liz returned to the case asking Joe if the Jane Doe was on a missing person's list.

"We are waiting. Her face is being checked now."

"Maybe she's on a passenger list...Greyhound, airlines, Amtrak."

"You mean give her mug to the travel industry?"

"Is that possible?"

"Yes. Only it doesn't explain luggage. Where would her luggage be?"

"Killer?"

"Couldn't get rid of it very easily. And someone would see, notice I would think. Not a tidy situation."

"Or it could already be at a hotel. She may have already checked in somewhere."

"Liz, you're a genius. That is definitely something to look into!" Joe again sounded satisfied with this tiny increment.

For the remainder of Friday evening and then the whole weekend, Joe seemed to have the weight of the week off his shoulders. He told Liz to look into a flight to Savannah sometime in October.

Joe relaxed and listened to his favorite music. Tonight it was Samuel Remy singing selections from Rogers and Hammerstein shows: *Carousel's* "You'll Never Walk Alone," *Oklahoma's* "Oh, What a Beautiful Mornin'!" and "Some Enchanted Evening" from *South Pacific* to name a few.

Liz told herself to allow more shoptalk during leisure times in the future. The investment was paying off!

Chapter 23
Shocked to the Core

"Dearie, you look jus' lovely! I've been so happy with Michelle at the salon; she's a darling, too, isn't she?"

"Very nice, Charles. I will be sure to ask for her next time I need a manicure or pedicure."

"Wonderful…see you soon!"

Patricia stepped out onto the promenade. She glanced at her watch…12:35. *Should I have lunch or head back to the spa and make myself a bite to eat?* The sun was very hot. The temperature indicated ninety-three degrees on the kiosk thermometer sitting on the grassy center strip of the promenade like a green backbone and just down from the salon and in front of the health food store. *The temperature sure has risen in a few hours.*

Oh, there's Erik. I didn't think he would be here today.

In a matter of seconds, Patricia was shocked to her core. Erik and a woman were standing just under the awning that announced "Be at your Best Health Foods Store." They stood in the shadows away from the bright sun, but from Patricia's vantage point across the street, she had a clear view.

She began to walk across the promenade, taking a few hesitant steps. This time, however, she was not looking at her toenails glittering with a new pink iridescence. She was looking at Erik. He appeared so much taller than the woman, blonde about five feet three wearing a denim miniskirt and red halter-top…very busty, too. Patricia suddenly stopped in her tracks. A passerby swerved quickly and sidestepped Patricia, having not expected such a hasty halt to this woman's gait.

Erik placed his arm around the woman. He leaned over. She stretched to meet him. His left hand moved to the back of the woman's neck. The woman met Erik's lips. They kissed.

This is no mere acquaintance! Patricia was too shocked to react with anger, surprise and confusion, yes. Patricia turned quickly and headed in the opposite direction. She hoped Erik had not seen her.

Fresh flowers for the reception area were out of mind now. The drive down GC1 to the spa seemed to take forever. She found herself having to check the speedometer. Anger was in view and not the roadway. When Patricia arrived back at the spa, she opened a note from Hans. "Will call on you around 2:00 p.m. Like to buy you lunch." *That certainly sounds good.* She felt the company of a man would do her some good at this point. *Half hour to spruce-up.* Patricia asked Louise, one of her most trusted employees, to handle the desk until 4:00.

"Ah…come to think of it, wait until I get back. I can't be sure when I will return."

Patricia hoped her being upset would not show. With Hans being very protective of both Angela and Patricia, Hans could kill Erik if he knew of this betrayal.

Chapter 24
"Another time, Hans, another time."

"Do you think he's unfaithful, Patricia, or a moment of weakness? I say, you know how I feel 'bout Erik."

"Hans, please. Don't judge so quickly."

From the third-floor outdoor café at the Hotel Gran Costa Meloneras, Patricia took a deep breath, soaking up the fresh air and a view of the sand dunes just below the terrace café. She looked and saw beyond the golden sandy beach of Maspalomas.

Hans Becker attempted contrition, empathy, and affection. "Look, I know I'm not one to speak 'bout fidelity.

But with Erik…I can speak 'bout his contributing to the operation…you know…I mean the spa. You work hard… and Angela…vell, Angela she work hard also in another way, the selling part, I mean."

"Take your order? Señorita? Señor?" The waiter at the hotel's café hesitated, knowing he interrupted a private conversation.

"We will boat have the lunch special, the fish of the day with mojo," said Hans.

"*Muchas gracias.*"

Hans looked affectionately at Patricia. "I care 'bout you, Patricia; I do not want to see you get hurt."

Patricia doubted Hans' sincerity.

"Care about me? Didn't you come to Gran Canaria hoping to find Angela…thinking she still had any passion for you?"

Hans leaned forward and said, "I admit. I'm sad that Angela is not here. But I am sincere with you."

Patricia's downcast eyes finally lifted off the lavender tablecloth. She looked at Hans, interrupted for the moment by a swift breeze that raised the edges of the tablecloth. Patricia and Hans clutched hands across the table.

"My affection for you is not like the wind, Patricia. It is steadfast."

After a moment's pause, Hans continued to gently squeeze Patricia's hands and said, "Confidentially, I'm retiring at end of this year. I want to settle here on Gran Canaria. I want us to be friends."

"What about your wife?" Patricia still questioned Hans' sincerity.

"It is over between Claudette und me. I will continue to provide if necessary. But this is where I want to be."

Their hands separated. Hans leaned back in his chair and looked up at the clear blue sky.

Patricia pulled back and said, "Hans, I don't think Angela cares for you any longer. Do you realize this?"

Hans looked at Patricia. "Yes, I can accept. I'm not coming because of Angela. I'm coming here because I want to, regardless of Angela."

Hans added firmly, "Und you…if Erik is no good for you then…I suggest a divorce."

"I can't just divorce him, Hans."

"If you need a detective, I will pay for one. Then you will know if he has been unfaithful."

Patricia thought the detective solution too extreme.

"Let me first see what I can get from him. I may even ask him about what I saw in front of the health store."

"Have it your way. But I leave Tuesday, Patricia. I can help you less after then."

"Let me think about it."

Patricia glanced at her watch, "Hans, I must get back to the spa. Drop me off; I don't think it would be good right now for Erik to see you and me together."

"But our lunch?"

"Another time, Hans, another time."

Chapter 25
Little Clues Can Add Up

It was Monday morning, August 25 in New York City. The heat wave had returned to the eastern coast. Joe MacLean and Hal Sweeney faced a tough week. Plans included checking trains, planes, buses, immigration, missing persons, hotels, as well as forensics for fingerprints, teeth, or any other possible venue in an attempt to identify the Jane Doe.

On the sidewalk outside BXTF, Joe lingered chatting with Detective Will Grogan. From the parking yard, Hal approached, having arrived a few minutes after Joe.

As Hal neared the two detectives, he noticed the lively conversation.

"…and I tell you, Will, I hate to fly. But sometimes you have to take the missus' point of view. And I'm looking forward to finding out more about Johnny Mercer. He was from Savannah, you know."

Grogan nodded his agreement about the missus. He had no idea who Johnny Mercer was. Joe and Detective Grogan saw Hal walking toward them, treading carefully not to spill his coffee clutched in his right hand and obviously trying to shed the stiffness in his bones after his long drive to the police station.

"Hal, how was the drive in from Selden?" asked Joe.

"Will, how are you? Not too bad. Only one and a half hours today."

"I don't know how you do it, Blimp." Grogan was forty-five, stocky, and overweight. He lived in Yonkers, about twenty minutes away.

Grogan continued seriously, "Listen, before I forget. Jacobs found out that the corner deli on the promenade off Jerome was closed that night. The Owens woman was walking from the A&P a few blocks away. She now tells us that she did bump into a guy running up to the elevated tracks at about the time of the murder. Doesn't remember much except that he had long black hair and looked Latino or Hispanic."

"That certainly does add to what she told us. Thanks, Will," replied Joe.

Joe turned to Hal. "Hal, maybe we can combine this information with what we find out over the next couple of days."

Joe said to Grogan, "We're going to check every possible avenue to come up with an ID on the victim."

Grogan acknowledged Joe's determination with a nod.

Joe changed the subject. "Mercer, Johnny Mercer, Will! He wrote 'Moon River,' 'Days of Wine and Roses,' and…and…'Ac-cent-tshu-ate-the positive, eliminate the negative.'"

"Yea…that's surely something we poor slobs have to do in our line of work, huh?" Will Grogan's smile filled his whole face.

Hal and Joe had a good laugh.

Hal's thoughts were already on the day ahead.

"Joe, remember? Van Bergen said they found black hair not belonging to the victim on the body."

Hal took another sip of his coffee. Joe could taste the Arabian Mocha waiting for brewing once he reached his office.

"Right, that's right. Little clues can add up, can't they, Will?" said Joe.

"Got to run, Brennan wants me to meet Smith. We're doing a canvass on another homicide. No mystery here, bastard just shot his wife. Trying to find out if there's a history…you know, beatings…arguments…the whole nine yards."

After saying good luck to Grogan with his canvass, Joe and Hal entered the precinct ducking under the "crucifixion" sign over the precinct's front door. They headed up to their second-floor cubicle.

After making a fresh pot of Starbucks coffee, Joe sat at his giant oak desk. *Let's see what's on the Internet that could help!* Hal, meanwhile, prepared photos for transmission to hotels, immigration, missing persons, the trains, buses, and planes.

By the end of the week, Friday, August 29, the information was out but there were no leads. No one recognized the victim. Angela Aquino lay on the cold slab—still a Jane Doe. Joe and Hal began to think this would be another long and drawn-out investigation. Forensics had promised something right after Labor Day, September 1. Joe and Hal arranged to stop at the NYPD Forensics Lab on Tuesday, September 2.

The killer had flown back to Barcelona. He then made the connecting flight and landed in Gran Canaria on Sunday, August 31.

Tupelos needed to plan a meeting regarding his next victim.

Chapter 26
Anxiety Squared

That's strange, no answer at Uncle Josie and Aunt Maria's. I guess Angela has them up and about town!

Patricia hung up the office phone at the spa. She worried. Angela wanted no one to know, but surely, by now she should have heard from her. Angela had always called on her birthday, even in times past when she was on holiday. It was now Monday, September 1 on Gran Canaria. Angela had left for Paris on August 13. While she had called from Paris when she was set to leave for the airport, thanking Patricia especially for the beautiful sweater, it had been… *almost two weeks and no word.*

Patricia used both hands to fluff up her hair. She had decided to give it some curl for a change. The fact was that Patricia had made herself unusually busy since Hans left to fly back to Stuttgart on Friday morning, having decided to spent an extra three days. Hans had avoided Erik and Erik stayed clear of Hans.

*****

"Hans, I appreciate your help and most of all, your presence these last few days. Angela not being here…Erik, that situation in front of the health store. This was your holiday and you devoted a good part of it to me and my loneliness."

"I would do more if you let me. You don't want my assistance…I can help by…"

"Hans, please. If I need your help, I will call. Even if is just to talk."

"Very well. Und here is my number. Claudette and I no longer live together. I am staying at the Golden Leaf Hotel, Stuttgart, Room 102. It's on Schutzenbuhl, Number 16. I chose it because I can walk from there to my office. Very quiet street, too, no vehicles, only pedestrian traffic. Should I change residences I will let you know."

And so it was between Hans and Patricia.

*****

On Saturday, Patricia had her nails done again even though they did not need it. She had her hair styled. She bought fresh flowers for the spa. She did clothes shopping—a busy Saturday and then Sunday to be sure. Now on Monday, she began to feel lonely again. She still had not confronted Erik. She was not sure she was up to it.

Patricia kept herself busy all Monday, cleaning and fidgeting around the spa. Erik was not around. Now Patricia did not like the images racing through her head—*Erik with that woman or Erik at the gym? Where?*

Erik was in Las Palmas.

"Listen, Bridget, I can't linger here too long. I must get to the gym. I'll see you again in few days."

"You're eager to build up a sweat in this heat?"

"No, no, it's something else I have to look into."

"Well, ok. But remember you promised me."

"I know, I know. It will all work out. Just give me some time."

Erik bent over and with his left hand on the back of her neck, pulled Bridget firmly towards him. She met his lips and they kissed.

Erik crossed the promenade. He entered the fitness center. Miguel was helping a big guy at the desk. Erik moved towards the desk; agitated, he blurted out, "Miguel, any messages?"

"Just a second, I have to take care of this gentleman first. Be with you in a few minutes."

"It's a simple request, Mickey!"

"Hey, Mack, he's helping me. Wait your turn." The guy was bigger than Erik was in height and bicep, weight, and calf.

"Fuck you, junior."

The guy turned, his face red like a blazing oven. "What did you say?"

"Hold on, hold on, gentlemen…no need for trouble." Miguel darted from behind the desk and got in between Erik and the big guy.

"Here. This is the message, I wrote it down again. This time it's just a number…no explanation."

Miguel handed Erik a note. He made a quick turn and stopped the big guy's advance on Erik. Placing his hands on the fuming big guy's chest, Miguel pleaded, "Go, Erik. You got what you came for." The words almost seemed to bounce off the huge guy's muscles.

"Erik, huh. That's the asshole's name?"

Erik turned, unconcerned at the threat and headed for the front door, ignoring the large guy's remarks. He stepped outside and onto the promenade to read the note. As the full sun shone on Miguel's handwritten note…Again, it was a phone number: 1-355-209-2930. A puzzled look crossed Erik's face. *This is going to be a tough one to figure out.*

Chapter 27
A Breakthrough

It was Tuesday, September 2, the Bronx, New York, 9:18 a.m.

Joe and Hal headed for the New York City Police Department Forensics Laboratory out in Jamaica, Queens.

Labor Day in NYC had been crisp and bright. Many folks hit the NYC beaches in swarms, knowing summer was quickly ending.

Tuesday was another story.

"I guess we can always say we need the rain, Joe."

"Maybe so, but this rain is like water poured from buckets!"

As the interceptor's windshield wipers barely kept pace with the downpour and splashes of mucky water from eighteen-wheelers on the Cross Bronx Expressway, visibility was reduced to only a few yards; Joe and Hal felt sure the Ark would be around the next bend in the roadway.

Joe squinted. "Is that it, the Whitestone Bridge exit?" Joe had driven the route from BXTF to the Forensics Laboratory many times. Today, he just was not certain given the traffic, rain, and dark skies that blanketed the Bronx like a giant gray shroud. The usual twenty- to twenty-five-minute drive took almost forty minutes with an accident on the Van Wyck Expressway just before the Jamaica Avenue exit, prolonging the time. Hal called ahead and told Doctor Van Bergen they would be late for their 10:00 a.m. meeting.

"Glad to see you both made it in one piece, Detectives." Maybe because she contrasted so vividly with the gloomy weather, Joe and Hal thought Van Bergen especially beautiful this morning. Her hair was golden, lips were pink, eyes blue as the sky, skin soft like velvet, and the white uniform was neatly pressed and clinging in all the right places.

"Yes, here we are. You're right; it is very wet today. Hope you had no trouble getting in this morning, Doctor."

Joe felt an uncomfortable dampness lingering between the tan raincoat and his blue blazer. He lifted slightly the left then right shoulder of the raincoat hoping to create a space between the coat, his blazer, and his shirt.

Hal said, "You told us you may have a breakthrough in the promenade slaying. What can you tell us?"

Hal had removed his raincoat and his brown tweed sport coat. He rolled up his long-sleeve white shirt and reached for his pen and notepad he had placed on a nearby desk.

"I hope this is helpful. Let's go over to my work station and I'll show you."

Joe and Hal could not resist a brief look at Van Bergen's perfect figure as they trailed a few feet behind. After about ten yards, they stopped at Van Bergen's brown metal desk, the screen on the computer depicting a banded cigar and the name Penamil Gran Reserva, "Made Exclusively in the Canary Islands for People Who Want the Best."

Van Bergen pointed to the computer screen.

"There…the first part of the puzzle. The brand of cigar you found on the promenade." Van Bergen wanted Joe and Hal to share her satisfaction.

"Are you certain?" Joe felt excitement building in his chest.

"Yes, positive. And expensive! Conrad, our research man, says it costs about $10.00 per and is only sold in packages of twelve."

As Joe decided to shed his coat and blazer also, he said, "Hal, you got that. This doesn't fit our Bronx neighborhood, now does it?"

Hal made a few notes and shook his head indicating agreement with Joe's assertion.

"Next, let me call up this website, and I can tell you something about the dress your Jane Doe was wearing." Van Bergen sat at her desk.

The computer display spoke garden green with bright sun-yellow tints to the right top and middle of the screen. Quickly pink, blue, and yellow dot-like images floated within a white rectangle in the center of the screen; then a white square below the rectangle…then a photo of a pretty woman! On the top of the screen was "Zara."

It was the website of the Zara Clothing Company.

"Ever heard of this company?"

'No, but perhaps Liz and Linda have. It's a clothing store?"

Joe looked intently at the screen as Van Bergen called up "trends," then "stores," then "services."

"That's right. Very Spanish. Some stores here in the U.S. but chiefly in Europe."

Van Bergen turned from the screen and looked up at Joe. Joe resumed an upright position. She continued…

"This confirms the origin of the dress as having been manufactured in Spain. Remember?"

"Yes, we talked about that last week."

"There's more." Van Bergen reached for a manila folder next to her computer.

"Look at this report. You remember my mentioning of the strange fibers found in what was left of the bra?"

"Sure do." Joe sensed this was a bigger clue than the cigar and the dress.

"Well, Detectives…here in the report…it's money fibers…Euros!"

"Euros, not dollars? Must have just arrived then and no time to change the loot?"

Joe continued, saying to his partner, "Blimp, what do you make of it?"

"Everything is pointing to someone who didn't belong where she was murdered, wouldn't you say, Joe?" Hal took notes as he spoke.

Joe nodded.

"And there is one more thing, Detectives. I checked with Reynolds at the medical examiner's office. Your Jane Doe was a 34B, 24, 36."

"Ok, very nice indeed...but...?" Joe's words dangled like the professor coaxing the pretty coed for an answer.

"The bra was a 36C! She was concealing the money in her bra!"

Joe looked stunned. Hal looked up from his notepad.

Joe had never heard of this scenario. He pulled over a brown corduroy padded metal chair believing it was a good time to reflect.

Hal sat on the edge of Van Bergen's desk. "Joe, we found no purse, no wallet... whatever you call what women use…and now we discover she had dough stashed next to her boobs!"

"Now, maybe that **is** in keeping with the venue!" Joe exclaimed.

Joe then glanced at Van Bergen who was returning to normal color after Hal's "boobs" comment.

"And so what's the summary, Hal…What have we got?" Joe gave Van Bergen a reassuring smile trying to blunt Blimp's coarseness.

"Let's see…One, expensive cigar only sold in a pack that cost about $120.00; two, dress made in Spain; three, money, Euros that is, concealed in a bra; four, bra a size bigger than the Jane Doe."

Joe pondered the information and then said, "We need to think about this back at the office, Doctor. We have to say you and your staff have come up with some interesting information. Let's hope it helps."

As Joe and Hal reached the exit, Van Bergen was running to catch up.

"Detectives, Detectives, one more thing! I can't believe I almost overlooked it." Van Bergen, temporarily winded, grabbed onto Joe's left arm.

"What is it?"

"The sweater...the sweater, blue with a flower design!"

"Right."

"It is handmade. The flower is the mountain laurel. It is the flower of the Canary Islands." Van Bergen spoke the last sentence as if it was a revelation from a botanical guidebook.

"Wow, that's two strikes for Canary Islands—cigars and the sweater. Hal, again, I say not quite a match with our Bronx!"

The trail was getting less obscure to be sure. Evidence was building.

But the evidence was not building fast enough to stop a much-related crime about to be committed some 4,000 miles away.

That would be in Stuttgart, Germany.

Chapter 28
Down Payment

Tuesday morning, September 2, Gran Canaria

"Erik, what's your hurry? I'm tired and it's only 8:15. I need to speak with you about something…and, and you said you were going to trim the hibiscus bushes."

Patricia's anxious voice sensed that Erik was planning an early exit from their condominium just a few meters north on the GC1 from the spa facilities.

Ignoring Patricia's question, Erik stripped off his black boxer shorts, donned a yellow waist wrap, and headed for the shower.

"Erik, are you going to be away the whole day? The morning? I need to know!"

Erik had turned on the shower and leaned back into the bedroom. "Listen, Patricia, I have to meet a business associate at 9:30. I really need to get up to Las Palmas. It'll have to wait."

Business associate? Or the busty blonde?

"What business could you possibly be...talking... about...?" Patricia's voice trailed off as she heard Erik slam the shower door.

I will find out for myself then!

Erik jumped aboard his motorcycle, a black Honda Nighthawk, and in his usual style, made plenty of noise as he left the condominium complex. Patricia was often glad that she and Angela owned the four one-bedroom apartments, since the renters were not in a position to complain.

Patricia decided to dress inconspicuously. To hide her identity, she hurried over to Angela's apartment across the hall and after a quick search, found a black and white "babushka." *I hate these things, but he'll never recognize me in this, some jeans, and a plain white blouse.*

Patricia was about ten minutes behind. *If Erik were indeed meeting some 'business associate,' then he wouldn't show up on Calle Mayor de Triana and the health store.* As luck would have it, Patricia spied the Honda Nighthawk just a few meters ahead on the two-lane road. She slowed down. She made certain the three cars between her and Erik sufficiently masked the silver Volvo. Erik pulled into a parking spot just a block off the pedestrian Calle Mayor de Triana.

Patricia was not sure she wanted to go through with this. *I think I'll scream this time!*

To Patricia's surprise, Erik strolled past the fitness center, walked by the health foods store with not so much as a glance, and continued down the esplanade to where it met the busy automobile thoroughfare. He stopped and waited. He looked at his watch: 9:15. A wawa, as they are called, or small yellow bus that was a common means of transport in Las Palmas, pulled up. Erik hopped aboard.

That's it. No chance now. But why did he leave his bike and take the wawa?

Patricia decided to buy some fresh flowers for the spa. She did not want this trip to end in nothing more that a cat and mouse adventure.

Erik's circuitous route masked his destination. After only a few minutes, Erik exited the wawa in an area not advised for tourists, containing seedy bars and strip joints. The kind of places the handsome cabby had warned Angela about years before.

Here also were gay establishments catering to the growing trend on Gran Canaria as a haven for alternate lifestyles not as easily tolerated on the Spanish mainland.

Erik chose a heterosexual strip club, the Pony Express, decorated like a John Wayne western. At this hour, it was only serving drinks, no bumps and grinds until nightfall. Erik pulled out a bar stool and sat.

"I'll have a Bloody Mary."

Erik checked his watch, 9:35. *Shit, I am late! Or did I get yesterday's phone message wrong?*

"Name's Erik. I was supposed to meet a guy here about five minutes ago. Did anyone ask for me?"

"No, only you and another guy in the place." The bartender's eyes indicated the restroom at the back of the club as he prepared the cocktail.

Erik reached into his pant's pocket. He looked at the "phone number" Miguel had scribbled the day before when Erik went to the gym to check messages.

1-355-209-2930

That fuck Miguel better be right.

Erik waited. A few minutes went by. Erik finished his Bloody Mary and signaled for a second. Sweat was building up on his forehead and his palms were wet like clams. He kept his eyes fixed on the front door. *Shit, I missed him! Five minutes late and the bastard's cut out!*

Erik finished the second Bloody Mary in three gulps.

Then from behind and to his right, "Erik, how the hell are you?"

The young man was in his mid-twenties, about five feet ten, with handsome Spanish-like features. A ponytail bunched up his black hair, which was covered in part by a New York Yankees baseball cap. He wore blue jeans and a cream-colored tee. He was muscular like Erik. With his left hand and before Erik could react, the young man pointed to the Yankees cap.

"Nice, uh, my souvenir from New York?"

"Shh, not here…let's find a table."

As the two men pulled up a couple of chairs and sat at a corner table, Erik decided this had better be short. Erik reached into his tee's pocket and unfolded a small piece of paper.

"Here. Here is the address in Stuttgart. He's staying at the Golden Leaf Hotel on Schutzenbuhl. It's a few blocks from his office. You have to kill him as soon as possible."

"Listen man, what about the $50,000. I'm not doing this for a fucking $15,000 again!"

"Look, I have some money I conned from a transplanted *fraulein*."

Erik again reached into his pants' pocket. He showed Tupelos a wad of Euros.

"Consider this 5,000 a down payment. You will have to wait until this is all over. Then I'll pay you the agreed amount."

"I hope I can trust you," replied Tupelos.

Erik leaned across the table and spoke in a whisper.

"You have to make it look like robbery. Make certain they can't trace you. Shave your head, that long black hair is too noticeable. Skinheads are all over Germany. And this time, I don't give a fuck about victim identity."

Erik paused. "Everyone will know it's Hans Becker."

Chapter 29
The Skateboard

By the end of Labor Day week, Detectives MacLean and Sweeney were still chasing dead ends. Liz MacLean's suggestion to Joe about the Jane Doe and hotel IDs did not pan out. Eliminated by week's end were immigration, missing persons, and transportation hubs with trains and buses. Scotland Yard, Interpol, and the FBI checked Jane Doe's fingerprints.

"Joe, our victim had no criminal record. Clean as a whistle. Yet, it doesn't add up. Could not have been a victim of a simple robbery." Hal was frustrated.

"Then we come back to why she was in that promenade in the Bronx," said Joe.

"Cab companies, Joe. We have to figure a cab transported her, for a reason we still do not know."

Ok. Let's run her photo to all cab companies. Tell them to post it in their offices, lockers, ah…the damn toilets… whatever."

It was Thursday, September 4.

The NYPD was moving fast; the killer was moving like a cheetah 4,000 miles away.

*****

Tupelos landed in Stuttgart on Thursday noon, two days after he had met with Erik Ruegar in Las Palmas. He checked into the moderately priced Kongress Hotel Europe on Seimans Strasse. His first task was to check out the hotel and surrounding areas where Hans Becker was staying about three kilometers away from the Kongress Hotel.

Public transportation in Germany was perhaps the best in the world. In Stuttgart, especially, the underground was the way to go. Vehicular traffic could add twice the time to a trip across town. It was ironic in that Stuttgart was the home of some of the most prestigious automakers in the world such as Mercedes-Benz, Daimler Chrysler, and Porsche.

The public system also assisted the criminal determined to exploit the anonymity of public transportation. In this city of almost 600,000 people, it was not difficult to move without detection if you were not in a registered automobile, that is.

Modern Stuttgart was a contrast of old and new. Old were the festivals such as Octoberfest and the wine festival, "Stuttgarter Weindorf," in August. Renaissance and neoclassical castles such as Hohenheim were rooted deep in history. The local mineral spas produced twenty-two million liters of water per day. At a Stuttgart open market, one could purchase every item from fresh vegetables and fruits to horsemeat.

However, here also were ultra-modern hotels and silvery corporate headquarters looking as if they inspired the computer age. Stuttgart also had beautiful parkland. In fact, twenty percent of the land was protected open space.

Housing architecture was a contrast. Many buildings dated before WWII, some obviously rebuilt due to heavy war damage while others were only a generation new. A mountain of WWII debris called "Bernkenkopf" or Rubble Hill was just outside the city. The war destroyed forty-five percent of Stuttgart.

Stuttgart pioneered the pedestrian precinct in the 1950s. Today, Konigstrasse or Kingsway was one of the longest at one kilometer and most sophisticated with specialty shops, department stores, cafes, and restaurants. The city, nestled in the rising slopes of the River Neckar Valley, enjoyed a relatively mild winter climate contrasted with most of Germany. "Swabian" was the term for local food and the dialect.

Hans Becker had announced his retirement upon returning from holiday in the Canaries. He agreed to stay on through March. Giving special talks to select visitors at the Porsche Museum proved exciting, a pleasant way to ease out of the company he had been at since 1965.

All at Porsche recognized Becker's knowledge about the company's history. Considered an expert in the evolution of Porsche's icon, the 911, Hans liked to brag, exaggerate really, that he saw all the Porsches built since 1948, over one million cars. Guided tours that took the visitor from early production to the choice of over 2000 custom paint colors took place at 10 or 2 each day. Hans' favorite color was Bahamas Yellow, originally found on the 1968 911L.

The museum, located next to the factory, was five miles from the city center. It was one-half mile from Hans' new residence, the Golden Leaf Hotel, a refurbished 120-room hotel located on a quiet pedestrian-only street. On the pedestrian avenue stood mostly older homes or two- to three-storied apartments with a Lutheran church at the end of the block. A two-acre park with stately elms, cobblestone walkways, well-trimmed shrubs, beautiful flowers, and globe-shaped lights marked the entrance to the quiet avenue, setting it off from busy nearby vehicular roadways.

It was not difficult for Tupelos to scout out the area, deciding the park would be the ideal place for the murder and robbery. He was now bald, carried a skateboard, and wore blue jeans, a tan pocket tee, and a black leather jacket.

The skateboard, not his usual mode of transport, was his only worry.

He did not want to fall on his ass.

Chapter 30
Going for the Jugular

It was now Thursday, September 4, Gran Canaria, 9:15 a.m.

"Erik, it's time we have a talk. I asked you for this time on Tuesday and you brushed me off." Patricia was determined to confront Erik.

"Yeah, I know. Well, what I had to do was important. I told you already."

Erik was wolfing down his usual breakfast of low-calorie eggs and turkey sausages. Patricia mulled over a cup of hot tea. They both sat at the small two-chair kitchen table. The sun's rays were bright through the small kitchen window. The condominium was of adequate size with a large master bedroom, living room facing out to the GC1 roadway, and small eat-in kitchen. To Patricia, it was home. To Erik, it was too confining. He wanted something better.

"Listen, our relationship is not the best these days. Frankly, I think it may be a good idea if we separate for a while," said Patricia.

"What's the problem? Listen, Patricia, we agreed a long time ago. You can do your thing and I will do my thing. Why are you questioning the relationship now?" Erik was dismissive.

Patricia's trusting nature had her tongue-tied for the moment.

As Erik got up to pour himself another cup of coffee...

"I noticed how cozy you were last week with Becker and..."

Patricia became red with anger. "Cozy? Hans was on holiday. He's thinking of moving to the islands. We had lunch; that's all, Erik."

Patricia went for the jugular. "And speaking of 'cozy,' I was in Las Palmas last week buying linens and getting my nails done. Do I have to say any more?"

Erik poured coffee. With eyes on the cup but with words directed at Patricia…

"What the hell are you getting at?"

"You don't know?"

After a sip of coffee, "Get to the point, Patricia!"

"Ok, I will. The blonde…I saw you with her in front of the health store."

Erik often mentally rehearsed his answers, ready for Patricia's doubts. He had anticipated that one of his meetings with Bridget might get back to Patricia.

"You mean Bridget, don't you?"

Patricia had gotten up from the table and was leaning with her back to the kitchen sink, her hot tea still steaming on the table symbolic of her growing anger.

"If that's her name…yes…yes…I do!"

Erik placed the coffee cup on the table. He turned toward the living room, walked a few paces, then turned back to look at Patricia.

"Look, it is business. I'm not happy being the security guard for the spa and a goddamn weed whacker. I want something more."

"You? Wanting something more? It seemed to me all you wanted was to grab her tits!"

"Very funny, Patricia. The fact is, I want to build a business. I want to combine a gym and the health store under one roof. It's a sure thing. Folks want good nutrition and exercise. I'm using the woman…that's all, Patricia."

Patricia was not convinced.

"And why did you leave your bike on Tuesday and take the wawa. What was that all about?"

"Shit, Patricia. Has it come to you trailing me now?"

"Tell me, Erik, because the next thing in this relationship is not going to be a separation. It's going to be a divorce."

Erik did not rehearse this one. He was less sure of himself.

"Business again. I had to meet this guy. He's a…a contractor…likes to hang out in the section of town where bikes can get vandalized or stolen. I didn't want to bring the bike down there…that's all."

"Contractor?" Patricia's tone was anything but that of one convinced.

"Yeah. The guy would remodel a gym. I've been looking at the one for sale over in the newer part of Las Palmas, to include the health foods concession."

"And when is this going to happen? And furthermore, where's the money coming from, Erik?"

"From the spa, Patricia. I was going to ask you to invest in the idea."

"Nice try. I don't control the spa, Erik. You know Angela has a say in the operations."

"Yeah, well, maybe you can convince her that it will be a good investment. She's the marketing expert. She'll see a nice connection between the spa and the health food/gym concept."

"We'll see, although I doubt it."

Patricia went from anger to anxiety.

Patricia's worry over not hearing from Angela prompted her to violate Angela's wish not to tell anyone of her trip to the United States.

"Speaking of Angela, I am worried. I have not heard from her since she left. She didn't want anyone to know, but she wasn't solely on a marketing expedition. She went to the U.S. to visit relatives. I don't know what to do? I did try to reach Josephine Valencia in New York."

Erik had to be cautious. He did not want to give away that he knew about the trip, having overheard Patricia and Angela arguing in Angela's condominium across the hall. Patricia had loudly admonished Angela for planning to carry so much money on her person. Angela then said she would conceal it in her brassiere.

Erik decided to respond to Patricia, worried that another call by Patricia to the relatives in the United States would upset the plan.

"The day you and Becker were out to lunch?"

"Yes, what about it? You were in Las Palmas," said Patricia.

"I was but I got back. You had Louise at the desk."

"What are you getting at, Erik?"

"Angela didn't exactly want to tell me anything. I told her you were out with Hans!"

"What? What are you saying? Angela called and you suggested I was with Hans! Didn't you explain?" Patricia expressively dumped the remainder of her cup of tea into the sink. "That's it? Did Angela say if she would call again?"

"No, again, she seemed in a hurry. Told her I would tell you she was ok."

"Can Louise confirm this?"

"No…she had left the desk for a short time. I took the call, didn't tell Louise about it."

"And didn't see fit to tell me either!"

"I'm not supposed to know where she is…so I left it alone."

"And did you know from the beginning where Angela was going and why?"

"No!"

Erik had done a masterful job of lying.

Shaken was Patricia's trusting nature. The Bridget incident had caused doubts. Again, Patricia's naiveté was her downfall. It did not occur to Patricia that Erik was lying about Angela.

Chapter 31
Sherlock Holmes?

It was Saturday, September 6, or two and a half weeks since Angela's murder. On Monday, Joe and Hal would testify at the preliminary hearing for Simmons, the person who confessed to the Latino girl's murder some nine months ago. On Friday, they assisted Grogan and Smith with canvassing a murder that had occurred at a Jewish deli in the Bronx on Featherbed Lane. The elderly owner was robbed and shot to death. There had not been much time to think about their Jane Doe case for the past forty-eight hours.

It was a warm morning as Joe MacLean lounged around the house, putting off cutting the grass for a cool breeze that never came. He plopped himself in his favorite easy chair and began to read the newspaper. He and Liz planned to take the kids to an afternoon matinee. *Stall this grass cutting long enough and I might just be able to put it off to tomorrow.*

Before the day was over, Liz MacLean would do some detective thinking of her own.

The phone rang. Joe feigned work.

"Liz, would you get that please? I'm heading out to the garage!" Joe felt so lazy he did not want to bother answering the phone.

Liz answered the phone in the front vestibule. She called out, "It's Lieutenant Jeffries, honey. He says he has to talk to you right now."

"All right, all right."

Joe glanced at the phone charger next to the easy chair.

Where is the cordless? Never in its cradle. Joe got up and strolled, annoyed, to the wall phone in the kitchen.

Joe sat on the kitchen stool in the recently remodeled kitchen. He rested one elbow on the new marble-top counter.

"Hello, MacLean here."

Jeffries called from BXTF where he was following up on Grogan and Smith's investigation.

"Listen, Joe, sorry to disturb you on your day off…but I think you and Blimp should know that this just came into the station regarding the Jane Doe murder."

"Really…well, is it a big break or just a little teaser?" Joe sounded mildly annoyed.

"That depends on the follow-up you and Blimp will now have to do on Monday," replied Jeffries.

"Lieutenant, I remind you we have the Simmons hearing on Monday."

"Fine, fine but you need to follow this also."

Joe stuck his tongue out at the phone.

Sitting in his new kitchen, Joe could picture the bill for the remodeling work. *No time to piss off the boss. I need my job.*

"Ok, what is it?"

"You got a match at a Jersey taxi company with your Jane Doe. A cabby says he recognizes the photo. Says how could he not?! She was very beautiful! Had several good looks at her, you know…remembers the brown dress, the mandarin-style collar, the blue sweater. Says she had a brown purse and a carryon, too."

"A carryon…that must mean…"

"You got it, Mac. Picked her up at Newark Liberty. Apparently, she had just come in on a flight that evening. She probably was uncomfortable with the cabby…didn't say much to him, only to take her to the Bronx, asked for Davidson Avenue….cabby couldn't find the street so, Mac,…get this…left her off on Jerome Avenue and 176th Street."

"That explains why the lady was in that neighborhood for sure. But did she tell the cabby what…I mean for what reason?"

"Nothing there. But, Mac, I have the company and the cabby's name. You and Blimp have to follow up on this ASAP. I mean Monday, of course. Find out what you can from the airlines. What flight came in around that time and from where?"

"Lieutenant…that would be Spain! We have enough already that points in that direction." Joe's faint smile hinted of future joy.

Liz had walked into the kitchen during the conversation. She could see Joe's excitement. She only hoped it would not interfere in their weekend plans.

"Great. Get on it right away. Monday, Mac! Take care and say hello to the family."

Joe handed Liz the receiver, motioning her to place it back in its cradle.

"Well, what is it?" Liz sensed a breakthrough.

"Seems we are a lot closer to identifying our Jane Doe. She came in on a flight from Spain, or at least that's a safe guess. Cabby in Jersey made a positive ID."

A light as bright as an interrogation lamp struck Joe MacLean's thinking. Having Liz standing there reminded him instantaneously of Liz's original thinking about luggage at a hotel. After straightening up first on the stool, Joe stood and paced the kitchen floor.

"Joe?" Liz wanted to be in on the insight.

"Liz, you remember your idea that our Jane didn't have any luggage and why not…because maybe she already had checked into a hotel?"

"Yes, I do. And now your going to tell me the cabby said she had no luggage…right?"

"The lieutenant, come to think of it, didn't mention that, but, Liz, that seems to be the case. But…she did have a purse and a carryon and there was no trace of those at the murder scene. What do you make of that?"

Joe and Liz drew closer together.

"That she had something in the purse or carryon that was even more valuable than the money that was stolen?" Liz faced Joe, her blue eyes beaming.

"Keep going, keep going…you're on a roll!"

"She didn't need any more luggage because she was meeting someone and staying with someone?" Joe gently held Liz's shoulders.

"Keep going…!" Liz looked away gathering her thoughts.

"The killer took the purse and carryon because it held her papers or something that would tell the police who she was…" Liz and Joe's eyes met. "And the killer didn't want anyone to know who she was?"

Joe took a few steps back and turned away, looking through the kitchen window and the tall grass that would wait for another day.

Still facing the window, "Liz, if that is the case…and no one can say right now that it wasn't…then the killer had to know who she was and had to know she was going to the Bronx from the airport! He was waiting for her!"

Joe again faced Liz.

"Or, Joe, he followed her to the Bronx, to that Jerome Avenue promenade, you know a 'follow that cab' cloak-and-dagger."

Liz frowned immediately regretting the metaphor since that was exactly Jane Doe's weapon of death.

"Sorry, Joe, didn't mean to bring that part of it up."

The comment only made Joe think more deeply.

"That's ok. And, Liz, there is the possibility that the killer, think about this for a moment, that the killer was on the same flight. A woman at the scene, Owens is her name, says a Hispanic-looking man brushed against her in a big hurry to get to the El." Joe began to emphasize his words with hand gestures.

"You and Hal will need to check the flights that night that came in from Spain."

"Liz, Liz…not only from Spain!"

Joe now could see the computer screen on Van Bergen's desk, the website that had identified the banded cigar found at the scene of the murder…Penamil Gran Reserva—"Made exclusively in the Canary Islands for…the Best."

"Liz, she was from the Canary Islands. And, **and**…so was he!" Joe's faint smile became broader in its satisfaction.

Joe was feeling like Sherlock Holmes, with the help of his wife, of course!

Chapter 32
Sensitivity Training

It was Monday afternoon in New York, a week after Labor Day. The Simmons hearing lasted until 11:30. After a Subway sandwich lunch, Joe and Hal headed out to Hoboken, New Jersey to interview the cab driver who had identified their Jane Doe from the circulating photos and sketches.

Mohammed Hakim was an immigrant from Kuwait. He lived on the third floor of a four-story brownstone on Ross Avenue just off Kennedy Boulevard, the main street of Hoboken, across the river from New York.

Joe was driving the interceptor as Hal looked for convenient parking.

"Hal, I thought parking in the Big Apple was bad. This is brutal. See anything at all?"

Joe saw nothing but cars and delivery trucks on the narrow side street.

"Joe, pull up there near the curb. We have an NYPD decal after all. I can't see the Hoboken cops making a fuss over it." Hal grunted.

Hakim had Mondays off. NYPD had informed him that homicide detectives would have questions for him sometime that afternoon.

Joe and Hal knocked on the third-floor entrance door at 1:10 p.m.

"Mr. Hakim, it's the NYPD. We are here to ask you some questions."

"Just a second, Officers." The deep voice came from behind the apartment door.

Three kids, ages about seven or eight, raced down from the fourth floor and flew like scattering birds past two of New York's finest in their scamper to the street.

"Jesus…Joe, shouldn't they be in school?"

Blimp looked over the banister and down the stairwell aperture.

"And I suppose we must look like truant officers from the way they went down those steps." Joe's words muted as the apartment door opened wide.

"Yes, I am Mohammed Hakim. Come in, please. Kindly remove your shoes, please."

Joe and Hal removed their shoes. Hal worried that his perspiring feet would stink. Joe took a glance at Hakim's slippers.

Hakim was a big man with a deep, bass voice. He was about six foot one, of solid build, mostly bald, had a thin black mustache, round face, friendly smile, and unusually large hands. The handshakes were firm.

Joe and Hal had received sensitivity training in the customs of Muslims since the flare-up over FBI rudeness following the attacks of 9/11. At that time, some agents had stormed into several Muslim homes and apartments on flimsy excuses based on "tips." Uproar in the Muslim communities throughout Northern New Jersey had caused serious backlash about FBI tactics.

Joe and Hal did not want the NYPD, at least in this small way, to add any fuel to the jihad fire.

"Hello, I am Detective Joseph MacLean. This is my partner Harold Sweeney. We are from the New York City Police, homicide investigation unit. We are assigned to the South Bronx." Joe believed he could not have been any more polite.

"Come. Come in and sit down. Over here in the kitchen."

Joe and Hal walked in their stocking feet, noticing the colorful oriental carpet in the living room and the prayer rug facing the eastern side of the room.

As Joe and Hal followed Hakim into the kitchen, Joe commented, "Mr. Hakim, we know you have already been most helpful."

As Hal went to sit down, Joe continued, "But we need to ask you some questions about the woman you transported to the South Bronx on the evening of August 19th."

Hal took out his notebook saying, "May I?" as he went to sit down at the kitchen table that looked very "retro" and definitely atypical in contrast with the heavy mahogany furniture in the living room.

Hal reflected with his usual cynicism, *Second-hand crap, no doubt.*

Joe remained standing. Hakim stood and faced Joe.

"How can I help you?"

"Did the woman have any luggage or did she say anything about where she was from?"

"She did not have any luggage. As I told the sergeant who took my call, all she had was a purse and small tote, as you say, or a carryon, I suppose it could be called."

"Did she say anything about where she came from or where she was going?"

"No…she did say, however, that she was happy to get a cab so quickly, given the rain and given the delays at the airport."

"Are you aware of any kind of delays she may have been referring to?"

"She was coming from the luggage area. Perhaps that was what she was talking about."

Joe looked over at Hal sitting at the chrome-legged and faux marble-top kitchen table.

"Hal, we need to check into that. Find out if any flights reported luggage delays…"

"Ok, got it, Joe." Hal smirked as he imagined all of the airlines having luggage arrival delays.

"…And, Mr. Hakim, do you know why she wanted to go that section of the Bronx?"

"She said nothing about that."

"Are you sure she asked you to bring her to Davidson Avenue?"

"Yes, I was not familiar with the area. I have only worked for Metro Cab for two months. I am sorry I couldn't find the street."

"But, Mr. Hakim, why did you leave the woman off where you did, on Jerome Avenue, is that right?"

"She had an address. She told me that her directions said that Jerome Avenue and Mount Eden were nearby where she wanted to go. When I found Jerome and 176th Street, she told me to leave her off there. I then told her to check with a local."

"Did you see anything unusual where you left her off… any men, specifically with black hair and probably Hispanic or Latino?"

"The rain was getting heavier. She paid the fare. As she was leaving, she pulled a sweater over her head as a kind of umbrella. I took one more look at her and took off. I didn't see anything unusual. It was kinda deserted."

"She didn't give you a specific address on Davidson, Mr. Hakim?"

"No. All she said was Davidson Avenue between 175th and 176th. So when I found Jerome and 176th Street, I figured it was pretty close by."

"I see. Well, Mr. Hakim, you have been very helpful. We thank you for the information."

Joe and Hal had their next stop. The drive to Newark Liberty International Airport would take thirty minutes from the Hoboken brownstone.

As the two detectives reached their illegally parked police interceptor, Hal grunted, "Jesus H. Christ, Joe, the Hoboken cops gave us a parking ticket!"

Chapter 33
Violet Dominated the Sky

In Garcia Tupelos' big hurry to get his hands on the 50K, he would get careless in his plan to rob and murder Hans Becker in Stuttgart.

After following Becker for two evenings and a day, Tupelos determined to act on the evening of Saturday, September 6 or at the latest, Sunday evening the 7th.

"You have to do it quickly," he recalled Erik Ruegar's instructions.

On Saturday night, Becker was planning to meet some friends a few blocks beyond the park entrance to the pedestrian enclave. The friends had decided to treat Hans to an opera, Bizet's *Carmen*. Showtime was 8:15 p.m. The friends originally said that they would pick Hans up in front of the Café Fulger, not far from the park entrance. But they changed their plan and decided to walk to the Golden Leaf, cross the park, and enter the pedestrian-only Schutzenbuhl.

As it would turn out, the friends' change of plans would thwart Tupelos' neat escape plot.

It was 7:35 p.m. Violet dominated the sky. Hans emerged from the Golden Leaf Hotel. He turned to his right and began to approach the neighborhood park about thirty yards from the hotel.

Tupelos was in the park practicing his skateboarding techniques, at one point, much to the hilarity of several teenage skateboarders who skirted through the area.

The park was in twilight. Tupelos had hoped for more darkness. He had already observed in the short time of stalking Becker, the auto executive's promptness and his desire to take in dinner around 8:00 p.m. Tupelos was confident that he could approach Becker in the park either at that time or later if necessary upon the latter's return from dinner. *Go with the flow, see what develops, but do it soon. If not tonight, then Sunday!*

Hans dressed smartly in a black tuxedo, pale blue tuxedo shirt, black cummerbund, black tie, and black leather shoes. No rentals here, Hans owned three tuxedo ensembles.

As he reached the park's perimeter, Hans acknowledged an elderly couple emerging from the park, *"Gute Nacht."*

The couple had just thought it odd to see the bald, leather-jacketed, mid-twenties young man trying his luck at skateboarding.

Translated: "Seems a bid old for that kind of stuff, don't you think, Gert?"

Hans looked forward to the opera. He preferred *Carmen* because the opera was set in Seville, one of his favorite destinations.

Tupelos' fumbling and stumbling with the skateboard turned out to be an ideal tactic in approaching Becker.

Tupelos came within a few feet of Becker.

Translation: "Oh, so sorry. Still don't have the hang of it. It's the way to get around though, better that the auto, don't you think?"

Becker used English: "Aren't you a bit old..."

Suddenly, Tupelos plunged the knife into Becker's right side having hoped for a chest blow. Becker pointing to the skateboard with his left arm, however, partly blocked the left-handed thrust by Tupelos.

Becker fell to the cobblestones. Tupelos drove the knife one more time into Becker's upper left thigh. As Becker lay bloody, ebbing strength still allowed him to block another blow to the chest.

Tupelos had to think quickly. People were approaching. *The old bastard will bleed to death; get the money, make it look like robbery...Get the fuck out of here!*

249

Tupelos used the bloody knife to cut the trousers. He snatched the wallet from Hans' left rear pocket. In a few seconds, he was on the skateboard darting from the scene.

But there were witnesses.

"Oh, my god, did you see that, someone has attacked Hans. He's down; let's hurry."

John Baxter and Bart Daniels, with their spouses, were Americans visiting Stuttgart for a few days. Both were American Porsche dealers from New York. They had decided to spend part of the late summer in the Swabian Forests.

The dealers had known Hans from his earlier visits to dealerships in the United States. He had helped introduce the Boxster model to American dealers. The Bizet opera was Baxter and Daniels' treat to Hans. They had decided, however, to walk to the Golden Leaf and meet Hans there, leaving the car behind with their wives.

"It was that guy on the skateboard, Bart!" Daniels shouted.

"Hans...Hans!" Daniels knelt next to the severely wounded man.

"He's losing it quickly, Bax. You stay with him. I'll get the police."

This time, there were witnesses, albeit at a distance. The police soon would have more, a knife found at the perimeter of the park.

Future tests would link the knife to the murder of Angela Aquino.

Chapter 34
No One above Suspicion

Joe and Blimp discovered the biggest luggage delay on the night of August 19 was at the Air France gate. The flight originated in Paris. However, with the flight originating in Paris, the crime's circumstantial link with Spain became shaky.

The two women and one male at the luggage claim area at Newark Liberty, Air France arrivals, readily spoke about the evening of August 19.

"Yeah, man, it was one of our worst yet. Luggage turns up the next day on another flight. Seems the stuff never got on the plane at DeGualle. Never happens here, I can assure you, Officers."

The African-American male spoke confidently as the two women nodded their agreement.

"You were all on that afternoon, evening?" Hal addressed the younger of the two women attendants, a thirty-something Latino.

"No, Officer, only Nathan. We were not on duty that night. Nathan here told us about it."

The second woman, a matronly African-American, added, "Some folks livin' way out in Pennsylvania didn't get their luggage until Friday of that week. Jus' terrible."

"Well...Nathan, then, which flight was it? Where was it coming from?" asked Joe.

Nathan checked the log.

"Well, Of-fi-cer Mac-Lean?" Nathan peered at the badge still on the counter.

"Yes, that's my name."

"It was Flight 242 from Paris."

"Do you remember seeing this woman, I know it was some three weeks ago, but can you recall?"

Hal showed Nathan a picture of Angela.

"Oh my lord, that's terrible; don't look, Ladies. It's a crime scene photo."

Following Nathan's plea, the two women squeamishly turned away.

"Sorry, Ladies, here's a sketch you can look at," said Joe handing the older woman a police sketch of their Jane Doe. The women shook their heads in the negative.

Nathan added, "There was lot of confusion and angry folks that even'n. I can't say I remember. It won't take much though to track down the flight crew. Those folks may remember if she was on that flight."

It was good advice and, in fact, was the next planned stop in the investigation once Joe and Hal determined the probable flight.

Joe and Hal ambled up to the Newark offices of Air France on the second floor of the terminal. A thin bald man in his fifties met them.

"Well, Officers, one of the flight attendants lives right here in the metropolitan area."

Trying to make light of the seriousness of the investigation, the Air France official added, "Manhattan, just down the road from you officers over there in the Bronx."

Joe and Hal remained stone-faced.

"Do you have a name and address, sir?"

Joe's formal and firm tone changed the official's demeanor. The official frowned and went to his desk files.

"Jamie Bender…ah…433 West 48th Street. It says between 9th and 10th."

"You're certain Ms. Bender was an attendant on that flight?"

Hal sounded displeased with the Air France official's recitation of the personal information.

"I'm sure of it, Officers. She can probably help you. Shall I see if she is on a flight now or off duty?"

"No, that won't be necessary, thank you. Please do not notify Ms. Bender. We will take it from here," said Joe.

Joe's experience told him that at this point, no one was above suspicion.

Joe and Hal decided to give their wives a call. It would be a long night. They would drive over to Manhattan. Hot leads cannot get cold. If Ms. Bender was in town, Joe and Hal were determined to find her no matter what.

Chapter 35
Without a Response

Tupelos made his call to Gran Canaria from the Kongress Hotel on Siemans Strasse. He ditched the skateboard, deciding to take the underground. It was 10:15 p.m. in Stuttgart, 9:15 on the Canary Islands. He knew this one was not clean. The knife was gone. He wore gloves but he could not be sure. Were there prints on the knife handle?

He was particularly worried because he heard the shouts, "Hans, Hans is down. That guy, over there…" The rest had faded under the screeching of the skateboard on the cobblestones, then the leap off the curb, then the powerful landing on the macadam. *Shit, somebody was at the scene who knew Becker. Will they be able to identify me?*

Tupelos decided he was going to check out of the hotel immediately, that is, after a phone call to the Canary Islands. He felt like a fugitive, not like with the first victim. If he had to, he would spend the night in bars and cafés, get a flight out in the morning or maybe this time the train.

He made the call. Miguel had closed up the gym at 9:05 and was about to lock up for the night. He hesitated but decided to answer the phone, thinking that maybe it was his brother. They had planned to meet for a few drinks.

"This message is for Erik. Tell him I'm at 1-201-941-5145."

Miguel wrote the number on his yellow memo pad next to the gym phone.

Maybe because of fatigue or maybe because he felt used again by Erik or even because the number sounded familiar…like from the first strange message of three weeks ago…

Miguel said, "Yeah, one is an 'I' right?"

The caller hung up without a response.

"Bastard, you can tell Erik boy yourself!"

Chapter 36
Revealing Interview

Joe and Hal were on their way to interview the airline attendant who they hoped could move the investigation forward.

Jamie Bender had inherited the first-floor condominium on West 48th Street in Manhattan. Located in the Clinton section of Manhattan, the railroad flat had a typical front-to-rear floor plan: first, a living room with two double hung windows almost to the floor and with heavy security bars; next, a bedroom area large enough only for a Murphy bed and dresser; next, a small kitchenette and eating area; finally, a bath at the rear and a back door leading to a postcard-size but picturesque garden. The same was true for the apartment condominiums across the hall and on the second floor with the upper floors having small balconies instead of the garden.

Bender used her knack for interior decorating to make the condo into an attractive bachelorette retreat. The residents of the cooperative had worked hard over the last few years to rid the street of drug dealers and prostitutes. They credited former Mayor Rudolph Guiliani for the improvements.

West 48th Street was now well lit and safe. The building was a low-step white brick with no impressive entrance such as found on the west side. Similar structures flanked the building on both sides. The theater district roared only a few blocks to the east. A placement facility for disabled persons anchored the north corner of West 48th and 10th Avenue. A fenced-in hoops playground stood directly opposite on the south side of the street.

It was 4:15 when Joe and Hal were buzzed through the front door after entering the building and checking for Bender's name on the letterboxes. They identified themselves to a soft-spoken young woman on the other end of the intercom. The delicate voice would prove to be a good predictor.

Hal knocked firmly on the apartment door located on the west side of the building and in the middle of the tiled brown and beige corridor.

"Good afternoon, Ms. Bender?"

"Yes, won't you come in please?" Jamie Bender was a tiny, almost fragile brown-haired woman no more than five feet two and 105 pounds. She dressed in a yellow chenille robe with matching yellow slippers. A radiant tan acknowledged duty in sunny locales around the world.

Hal replied with a thank you and introduced Joe.

"We hope we are not intruding like this without notice, but we are investigating a murder and we think that you may be able to help us."

Joe's words seem unusually soft, even graceful to Hal, perhaps because of the nature of the inquiry but also, thought Hal, any tough, harsh questioning might blow over the wispy young woman.

"A murder? What would I know about a murder?" Genuine concern flashed across Bender's slender face.

Bender turned and motioned the detectives to the front of the apartment. As she led the detectives to the living room, she apologized for her appearance explaining she had no flights that day and had decided to lounge around the apartment.

"Ms.? Or I'm sorry, is it Miss? May I call you Miss?" Joe had not yet become comfortable with the Miss, Mrs., and Ms. salutations of the new age.

"Miss is fine."

"Thank you...Miss Bender, you could be very helpful, but this won't be easy."

Bender sat and crossed her legs leaning forward in the Queen Anne style chair. The robe separated strategically, exposing a tanned pair of legs. Joe continued.

"You were a flight attendant on a flight about three weeks ago...a flight from Paris to Newark. I am going to show you a few photos, I warn you they are not pleasant, but we want you to try to remember if this woman looks familiar to you. We believe she may have been on that flight. We know this because we have strong indication that she was delayed at the baggage claim and this flight...ah Air France Flight 242...had severe baggage issues. We know this from the Air France officials at Newark Liberty. The official gave us your name; that's why we are here. Please, do you mind?"

Joe motioned to Hal. Hal handed Bender the crime scene photos. After studying the photos for about thirty seconds, the tiny but obviously not squeamish young woman responded.

"You know, I see many passengers. And it's difficult to remember. But in this case, I recall...I remember...because of this woman, the woman here in the photos, sitting near the emergency door and by the window and an older woman sitting next to her, in the middle seat, and making a fuss over her husband not sitting next to her, on the aisle it was, but a few rows back. That would be, I think, row 32 or 33 on the Boeing model used by Air France. It's just funny...I do remember more the older woman and her husband. The husband took the seat next to his wife after I asked a man if he wouldn't mind moving so a husband could sit with his wife. I remember that because we all had a chuckle over the man's bladder problem, what I mean is he needed to sit on the aisle."

Joe and Hal were surprised at the relatively easy recall of the flight and the passengers.

"Anything else you can tell us, Miss Bender?"

"Let me think...Yes, I also remember that the older woman and this woman, in the photos, seemed to get along quite well. I remember them talking on the flight quite a bit."

"What about the husband?"

"No, not much, he read a lot, I think. You know, I'm surprised I remember this much. I usually don't."

"Now, Miss Bender, here is the million-dollar question! Did the woman in these photos seem nervous, suggesting perhaps she was hiding something or was running from something or someone?"

"Detective, nearly 200 people were on that flight. A lot of people are nervous on an airplane, especially since 9/11. It is my task to make them feel as comfortable and welcomed as possible. Frankly, she didn't seem nervous at all. I recall the older woman exhibiting more agitation than her."

"From what you have told us, you have a pretty good idea of where this woman...and the older couple, for that matter, were sitting in the aircraft. We can check the passenger list. It definitely was Flight 242 out of Paris?"

"That's right. It was a connecting flight for some. One of those tour groups you know. I remember talking to several passengers. They had all bragged about the August weather along the Mediterranean, said they were on a tour, and returning from Spain, Italy, and France. Somewhere like that."

Bender slouched in the chair, exhausted it seemed with the details she was recalling, but also with a satisfied look that she was being helpful to the investigation.

"We have reason to believe the woman in those photos was from Spain. Circumstantial to this point…the passenger list will give us a name." Joe sounded confident.

"There is a big caveat, Detective. I shouldn't admit this, but sometimes the airlines don't insist on passengers sitting in their assigned seats. At least that's the case with Air France. Like the older man moving to the seat next to his wife. That wasn't his seat. Of course, in case of a tragedy…" Bender trailed off not wanting to think of such a possibility.

"Yes, we get the picture. Nevertheless, this information will help."

Joe stood. Hal closed his notepad. Bender stood.

"Thank you. We feel we are close to identifying the victim thanks to the information you have provided us this afternoon."

Bender looked up at the taller detectives. "And the murderer? Who would do something like this?"

"Well, Miss Bender, we have reason to believe that the murderer was on the same flight with the victim. Again, only circumstantial at this point."

"Oh my, how awful. On the same plane…how terrible." Bender's eyes stared down at the floor.

"Yes, well, we are now going to have to check the passenger list. If we showed you a photo in a few days of the older woman, and the older gentlemen, who you have indicated sat next to the victim, do you think you can identify them?"

"Yes, I think I can."

Joe and Hal were very close. Victim identification was at hand.

Identifying the murderer, however, would take a trip by Joe and Hal to Europe. They would need the help of the Spanish National Police and Interpol.

Chapter 37
Grand Scheme Goes Awry

With Baxter and Daniels immediately at the scene of the assault and the quick attention by emergency personnel to Hans Becker's wounds, there was a good chance Becker would survive. He remained in critical but stable condition at Robert Bosch Hospital. The hospital, located in a park/campus setting, was only a few minutes from the scene of the stabbing attack. The ambulance had sped off Schutzenbuhl to Highway 10 and then onto Heilbronner Strasse. A jug handle took the ambulance onto Auerbach Strasse, the entrance to the modern healthcare complex that looked more like a vacation retreat with its reflecting pools, fountains, and manicured grounds.

Baxter had accompanied Hans to the hospital in the ambulance. His associate, Bart Daniels, and the two wives arrived at the hospital a few minutes later.

"Is there a wife or perhaps children who should be notified?" The thirty-something emergency surgeon put the question to John Baxter.

"Actually, we are not sure. Our understanding is that he and his wife, I don't even know her name, Doctor, have separated. My associate and I are Americans. We are here on vacation. We really don't know Hans that well."

"I see. Well, I'm sure the police will locate his family," replied the doctor. The doctor continued endorsing the quick action of Baxter and Daniels.

"Herr Becker had lost a lot of blood, your being on the scene so quickly after the attack probably will enable him to pull through."

Satisfaction mirrored in the two Americans' faces.

As the doctor began to leave the emergency room waiting area, the State Police of Baden-Wurttemberg arrived in the person of Helmut Bassen, the equivalent of an American homicide detective. Stuttgart is the capital of the German state of Baden-Wurttemberg and the headquarters of the Staates Polizei for the area.

After introducing himself to Baxter and Daniels, Bassen asked about the attacker.

"Gentlemen, what can you tell me about the assailant. We found the weapon, incidentally, and are running it now for prints."

Daniels spoke first. "He was about twenty-five or so, a white but I don't think Anglo, American, or even German. Bald wearing a black leather, I think, jacket over a T-shirt, didn't notice any color, and blue jeans. A big guy, well-built maybe more than six feet. Bax, here, and I had a pretty good look...What would you say, Bax, we were about fifteen yards away when it happened?"

"That's right. The guy sped away, if that's the right word, on a skateboard," added Baxter.

"If you were asked to look at photographs, do you believe you could identify the man?"

"Yes, I believe I could, if he is dressed the same," commented Daniels.

"And you, Sir?"

"I'm not sure, I was a few more yards away than Bart," replied John Daniels.

The information was far from conclusive, but it was helpful.

*****

Meanwhile, Garcia Tupelos had an uneasy feeling as he deserted the Kongress Hotel on Seimans Strasse, ironically, only a few blocks from the hospital where Becker lay fighting for his life. It was 10:10 p.m. He knew he had to get out of the country fast. The knife had his prints, he was sure of this now. And, given his arrest in Barcelona some years before and his fingerprints on record, he knew he had to go into hiding. But how to collect the money? Would Erik Ruegar claim no payment was due given this delay?

The cash in Becker's wallet would be enough to buy a train ticket out of Germany. That would be easy enough. He decided on Spain. He could not stomach any longer the rest of Europe. He wanted to be home, in familiar territory where he could hideout for a while. He did not dare return to his crumbling flat in Las Palmas.

It was in Las Palmas where he had met Erik Ruegar, lounging one night in a sleazy bar about a year and a half ago.

Ruegar had been drinking, complaining to anyone who would listen…

"She thinks I'm fucking useless, a weed whacker; thinks all I'm good for is cutting the bushes and looking out, well looking out for assholes like you…." Erik pointed a lazy finger to his left, to the guy next to him who was eyeing the shapely female bartender in her tight black pants.

"Hey, wait a minute," responded Tupelos who was sitting that night on the bar stool next to Erik Ruegar.

"Take it from me, all women, I presume you're talking about your wife, are problems. Me, I'm single and it's going to stay that way."

Tupelos stared at the bargirl now stretching up and reaching for a bottle of rum.

Then leaning into Ruegar, he said, "Look at that ass, nice ah?"

Erik ignored the observation and instead continued, almost with sorrowful expostulation, "I'm going to get out of this goddamn rut, I tell you I want my own business. I think guys and (looking now at the bargirl) dames like that would enjoy a gym where they can work out together. Look at me, I'm fit, work out, you know!"

"Plenty of gyms already, you need something different. I agree the sex thing will help bring them in. But you need a gimmick, like health food maybe."

Ruegar placed his Bloody Mary on the bar. He thought that this guy next to him was somebody who might help. After another fifteen minutes or so of chitchat, Ruegar and Juan Jose Garcia Tupelos launched the grand scheme.

The catch? Tupelos insisted it was going to cost $100,000. For that money, Tupelos would get rid of the people who stood in the way of big money and future plans.

*****.

Juan Jose Garcia Tupelos recalled the deal some eighteen months later. It had not gone quite the way he planned. He was confident, though, he could hide from the authorities for a couple of months. Ruegar would have to wait.

Another development in the grand scheme would also have to wait.

The wanted posters would be up in less than forty-eight hours!

Tupelos decided he needed a revolver.

Chapter 38
Long Black Hair

The Air France passenger list had turned up several potential suspects. Of the almost 200-plus passengers, twenty-eight males had given their addresses as Spain, three of these among the islands of the Canaries. The NYPD, with the help now of Interpol, were searching the databases.

Air France officials had identified Barbara Neldon, fifty-nine, of Leonia Park, New Jersey as having sat in row 32, seat B. In aircraft passenger records, a Frank Pastore sat in seat 32C on the aisle. The individual they believed who sat in row 32, window seat, was Maria Aquino. She had given her address as 303 GC1, Gran Canaria, Spain. Bender, the Air France flight attendant, had stated that passengers might not have sat in the assigned seats, making all the identifications tentative at best. Only a face-to-face interview would suffice.

It was now Monday, September 8.

Barbara and Cliff Neldon lived in a pleasant, although aging, Dutch Colonial on Longacre Terrace. Joe and Hal parked the Crown Victoria interceptor in the driveway, street-parking non-existent nowadays in the suburbs with almost every home having three vehicles. They pulled up behind a tan Saturn coupe. Both Neldons indicated they would be home and would be most willing to help.

"Hello, Officers, please come in. My wife will join us in a minute. Nice weather, isn't it?"

Joe and Hal sensed and expected uneasiness in Cliff Neldon's demeanor. The weather remark only reminded Joe of the long drive over the George Washington Bridge, the drive on the overcrowded highways leading out of NYC, the several straight days now of high temperatures and equally unpleasant humidity, and most of all, the fact that the interceptor's AC wasn't working again.

"Yes, it seems summer is going to be with us for awhile yet," commented Hal as he and Joe took a seat in the living room, part of a great room combining the living and dining areas.

"You have a nice home here, Mr. Neldon…ah, and is this Mrs. Neldon?" Joe stood. Hal stood. Mr. Neldon moved to the rocker by the summer-quiet fireplace allowing Barbara to sit in a high-back wing chair. The detectives returned to the three-cushioned Ethan Allan sofa decorated in the mountain laurel motif. Joe noticed the irony immediately. Hal was oblivious.

In the few seconds of transition, Joe pondered the blue handmade sweater with the mountain laurel design. He saw again the sweater covering the beautiful long black hair, the right hand clutching the sweater in a death grip. *The rude promenade.* He pictured the graffiti, the painted concrete, the three barely alive trees in the center of the promenade, the drizzle, the rain, the blood.

Hal waited a few more seconds for his partner to begin the questioning. Hal decided to say something, anything. He was not accustomed to the silence.

"Well, Mr. and Mrs. Neldon, we have some questions for you," started Hal as Joe gave the sense of being adrift in time.

"As you know from our phone call, we are here on a murder case."

Hal stumbled. He usually was not the talker. *I should be taking notes.*

"The woman…the women here in these photos," said Hal thrusting the crime scene photos towards Barbara Neldon, failing to warn her of the unpleasantness.

Joe broke from his funk.

"Yes, I'm sorry. Hal, please take out your notes on the case." Joe thought again…*Perhaps, I no longer believe in human goodness.*

Joe straightened up as best he could in the soft, cushiony sofa.

Barbara Neldon brought her right hand to her mouth. Anguish distorted her face, her whole body tightened at the horrific photos.

"Oh, Cliff, Cliff, please get me some tissues."

Cliff Neldon hurried to the bedroom just off the hallway.

"Well, Mrs. Neldon, is that the woman you were sitting next to on the flight from Paris about three weeks ago?" Joe was finally in the present tense.

Cliff Neldon handed his wife a box of Kleenex, looking over her shoulder at the photos.

"Oh my god. Is she dead?" Tears welled up as Barbara recalled the pleasant conversation, the sharing of dreams and experiences, the quick friendship, the strange mystery…the secret of the money.

"So that **is** the woman?" Joe sought closure.

Cliff Neldon spoke, rescuing his wife for the moment.

"Yes, that is the woman my wife sat next to. I sat on the aisle after moving from a few rows back."

"And you, Mrs. Neldon?" asked Joe.

"Angela…Angela…that was her name. Oh my god, what a tragedy. Murdered? Why?"

"Did you say 'Angela'?" Hal's confusion showed in his wrinkled brow and facial frown.

"I'm positive. We spoke at length. I'm sure of it." Barbara Nelson sounded certain.

"Her name wasn't Maria?" Hal sought clarification, something.

"Mrs. Neldon, was there anything unusual about her?" asked Joe believing they had the right victim regardless of the name confusion.

"Yes, there was. She was a wonderful, warm, friendly person. Said she lived in Germany for many years, said she owned a spa."

"Germany?" Hal was very confused at this point. *Angela? Germany?*

Joe could sense there was more to it. He pressed on.

"She wasn't German; we think she was Filipino."

"No…what I mean is she said that she was originally from the Philippines, moved to Germany, and then to the Canary Islands. Said she and her sister owned a health spa out there."

"On the islands, the Canary Islands?"

"Barbara? Barbara, the money!" interjected Cliff.

"Money?" It was Joe's turn to be confused.

Barbara looked derisively at her husband.

"Oh, Cliff, I don't think she was a criminal or something like that."

Barbara spoke calmly almost defending Angela's memory.

"Detective, what my husband is referring to...this woman was bringing into the U.S. lots of money. We know this because she showed it to me. She had it hidden in her...her...brassiere."

Hal thought, *That explains the cut bra.*

"Why would she tell you this? Didn't you think that was suspicious?" Joe regretted the tone but believed he had to probe.

"She had gotten through customs in France. With all the tightened security in the United States, she was worried that she would be caught. Said she was visiting relatives in the Bronx and the money was meant for them."

"Suspicious story? Didn't you think so at the time?" asked Blimp.

"No, like I said, this woman was on the up and up. I'm sure of it. I am naïve, I admit at times, but I know when people are telling the truth." Barbara spoke with assurance.

"Detectives, my wife is a very good judge of character. She knows good people when she talks to them, and she knows a phony."

Cliff came to his wife's defense, conveniently forgetting his usual lament regarding Barbara's ability to talk to almost anyone.

"It does add up."

Hal was looking at Joe, confident he had gotten it all straight at last.

"Mr. and Mrs. Neldon, we have reason to believe this woman's name was Maria Aquino. That she was murdered for that money...ah did she say how much it was?"

"She said Angela, not Maria; could it be the wrong person?" Barbara was in denial.

"Detectives, as a former school administrator in a predominately Spanish community, I can tell you that many, most even, of women of Spanish ancestry use Maria as a first name. It is respect for the Virgin. But the girls go by their middle or confirmation name."

"So her name was Maria Angela Aquino." Hal wrote it down.

"Getting back to the money, how much did she say?" Joe felt warm inside knowing their Jane Doe was no more.

"I can help there," said Cliff. "Our estimate was about $15,000 in American money. Her money was in Euros. I know because I asked my friends who were on the cruise with us about the amount and if it would be a problem bringing that amount into the country. They were sitting about ten rows in back of us."

"Are you saying that other people on the aircraft knew about this money?" Joe saw motive.

"I can assure you, Detective, our friends are good people." Barbara sounded indignant, and then continued…

"Cliff, didn't you say, though, that Ben…" Barbara redirected her words to Joe…"Ben was one of our travel companions…had spoken rather loudly about the amount and also to Arty's displeasure."

Barbara glanced at Hal and continued, "Arty is our other friend along with Beatrice. We call her Trixie. They all sat near the back of the plane."

"Let me understand you…" Joe sought clarification. "Your travel friends also knew that the woman was trying to get money by customs?"

"Yes, that's right. In fact…" Cliff Neldon stopped in his mental tracks. He recalled the olive-skinned, handsome youth, the cocktail on the plane, the one piece of luggage at the airport, and the long black hair passing their aisle on the way to the lavatory, the lingering at the airport…Was he waiting for someone?

"What is it, Mr. Neldon?" Joe recognized the spacey demeanor similar to his own distant thoughts at times.

"This could be far out, but there was a guy on the plane and later at the baggage claim area…"

"Yes?"

"Well, he seemed very interested when our friend Ben mentioned loudly the amount of money this woman had on her. And then later, he could have been stalking her at the airport. Wild, but possible."

"Can you describe this man?" asked Hal who was ready to write down a description for the police sketch artists.

"He was in his mid-twenties, I'd say. Handsome features. I would say Hispanic by his olive complexion, about six feet and maybe 185; very strong looking."

"Anything else?" Joe knew they were close!

"Yes, he had long, flowing black hair to the shoulders."

Joe and Hal believed they had their murderer. Whoever was in the seat forward to the Neldon's travel companions was looking like the perpetrator, seat 42 by the window. The NYPD would now look to Interpol for assistance.

Chapter 39
Interpol

Interpol headquarters was located in Lyon, France. The organization began in 1923 as the International Criminal Police Commission. It was then located in Vienna, but moved after World War II. The term "Interpol" was once the telegraphic address of the organization.

The responsibilities of Interpol were vast, but they all boil down to cross-border criminal police cooperation. There were 181 members including the United States, France, Germany, and Spain. All would soon be involved in the hunt for Juan Jose Garcia Tupelos.

Although not primarily an organization that would track down national-based criminals such as Tupelos, Interpol resources provided excellent fingerprint identification.

For Joe and Hal, this would be their first case involving Interpol.

The German police had traced Tupelos to the Kongress Hotel. Latent prints on the knife were matched with prints taken five years ago when Tupelos was arrested, but never convicted, for assault and robbery in Barcelona.

Though Tupelos did not use his real name at the hotel, it was not difficult to establish his identity thanks to prints found in the hotel room. By the morning after his quick departure from the hotel, the German police had a positive identification: Juan Jose Garcia Tupelos, a Spanish national.

Joe and Hal checked again with Air France. The man sitting in seat 42A by the window, the seat forward to the Neldons' travel companions, was identified as Juan

Tupelos. He had given this as his full name. He listed an address in Las Palmas, Gran Canaria.

As of the moment, the detectives were not certain if Tupelos fit the description given to them by Cliff Neldon. Joe and Hal needed a photo or very good sketch.

By Wednesday, September 10, they had their photo. Tupelos was on file with the Spanish authorities. A quick return visit to the Neldons that afternoon pointed clearly in the direction of Tupelos.

Unknown for the moment to Joe and Hal would be the killer's involvement in the Hans Becker attempted murder. That crime made Tupelos an even more desperate criminal, a criminal who now would not hesitate to shoot his way out of trouble.

Chapter 40
"I want this guy collared by NYPD."

To Joe and Hal's surprise, but to Liz and Linda's chagrin, Chief Brennan told his detectives to get their man **in person**. But where was Tupelos? Still in the U.S.? The chief was quick to surmise that the suspect had returned to Europe. The chief was right! Running Tupelos and his mug shot through airline records confirmed that Tupelos had indeed flown back to Spain.

"Get the first flight out to Barcelona, Mac, then to the Canary Islands. Interpol and the Spanish police will have something in a few days. Count on it."

Chief Brennan gave the two detectives plenty of reading matter for their trip to Barcelona. Brennan was an Interpol enthusiast: lots to read particularly about international cooperation and fingerprinting identification procedures.

Before their departure, Chief Brennan summoned Joe and Hal to his first-floor office in BXTF. Joe and Hal had to sit through a long-winded lecture by Brennan on Interpol procedures. It was the price for the taxpayer paid trip to Spain, albeit a potentially dangerous mission.

"Mac? Blimp? Let me assure you that you are working with the finest Europe has to offer when it comes to Interpol."

John Brennan was almost a look-alike to another Brennan, one Walter Brennan, the actor. The actor had died in 1974, but from his old movies on TV, Joe could see the similarities: the slightly raised upper lip on the right side of the face when he smiled, the bushy eyebrows, the deep furrows of the cheeks, the black eyes, even the gray hair. Joe never mentioned the similarity to Hal figuring Hal would only use it as an occasion to say something nasty about Walter Brennan. too.

"Why is that, Chief?" Hal felt the need to press Chief Brennan. *Does he really know about this, or is it more of his bullshit?*

"Maybe better than our F.B.I. with those idiot directors we've had the past several years, especially that guy Clinton appointed."

Joe shifted position in his seat opposite the chief's mahogany desk. The chief was always evoking the former president and always in the negative.

"You see with Interpol there is less politics. Their director is chosen by the member countries, not some politician like in Washington."

"Is that it, is that the only reason you think they are better than our F.B.I.?" Hal was pushing his luck.

"Of course not, Blimp. You see over there, it is the old school. Their fingerprint identification process is the way it's been for years, not this computer stuff that we're getting into over here. In fact, Interpol has established a standard for its members. Believe me, they have some of the best fingerprint experts in the world. How do you think they came up with this guy's prints so quickly?"

Brennan was not entirely right. Computers all over the globe are able to match fingerprints in a few seconds, even partial prints. What was part of the "old school" as the Chief understood it was that fingerprint identification was still the leading source of evidence in court, more than any other forensic techniques combined.

The chief was correct in another way: standards. With the move to an international standard, the exchange of evidential conclusions between countries was less prone to error or second-guessing, something that defense attorneys could then exploit; Interpol's adage—fingerprint evidence must be absolute with no room for likely or probable.

"Well, Chief. What you're saying is that we can be certain that Tupelos is our suspect. All we need to do is find him."

"You got it, Mac. Now, I suggest you make those flight arrangements."

The plane for Barcelona would leave at 7:45 Thursday morning, September 11. Rodrigo Vicario Sarova of the Spanish National Police would meet Joe and Hal at the airport.

The chief's final words could not have been more explicit. **"I want this guy collared by NYPD."**

For Joe, especially, the chief's emphasis would become an albatross.

Chapter 41
A Surprising Venue

Tupelos boarded the Deutsche Bahn (German railway) out of Stuttgart at 8:35 a.m. Sunday, September 7. His now dingy, unshaven appearance served as mask. He allowed the minimum necessities thrown into his satchel. Discarded items after deserting the hotel found their way into Stuttgart waste receptacles. No train connected directly to Barcelona. He would have to go first to Zurich.

The *Cisalpino*, a high-speed train, linked Stuttgart with Zurich, Switzerland. Knowing he was a wanted man, Tupelos had to think and act quickly. He decided on first class. He believed this would be a less likely tableau for his escape.

The bullet-nosed silver and gray *Cisalpino* express train with 475 seats could reach 180 miles per hour making the approximate 135-mile trip in less than fifty-five minutes. The problem: Tupelos' passport check as well as his ticket purchase would take place on board the train. He hoped he could at least flee Germany before detection. *One country at a time! Switzerland, then France, then Espana!*

Tupelos glanced eagerly through the complimentary newspaper, the *Stuttgarder Zeitung* on board. He also sipped his complimentary gin and tonic. He searched for any mention of the Becker attack in the newspaper. Since Becker was a high-level executive in the German auto industry, the press would surely cover his death. (He assumed Becker had died.) Nothing! After presenting his passport and purchasing his ticket, he asked the conductor if the train had any additional newspapers.

"Nicht!"

Perhaps there would be some news upon his arrival in Zurich.

The *Cisalpino* had 153 first-class seats; all with a table should the passenger wish to purchase a meal. Tupelos had no appetite. The oak laminated table only found pages of the *Zeitung* piled helter-skelter. The seat was extremely comfortable, expertly ergonomically designed. *Think I will try to catch a few winks,* thought Tupelos.

"Excuse, please, may I glance at your newspaper, the conductor said they were all out." The woman, about forty, spoke from the other side of the aisle opposite Tupelos.

"Oh, well sure. I didn't find anything interesting to tell you the truth."

Tupelos realized he spoke English in response to the English language request. Garcia Tupelos eyed the woman. She was fair-skinned with brown auburn hair and green eyes. Tupelos thought, *Maybe a few pounds too much on the body. Athletic though. Attractive face with straight nose, small mouth, and a pretty smile.* She wore a cream-colored V-neck top and brown pants.

"I'm so sorry. I am on my way to Lyon for a conference. I flew to Munich, bought this Europass. So here I am."

The train ticket rested prominently on the matching laminated oak table across the aisle and in front of the woman.

Tupelos did not want to get into any conversations. He would remain mute as much as possible. Courtesy, however, demanded a response for Tupelos was smart enough to know that rudeness would only make him stand out more in the woman's recollections of her vacation, trip, and business sojourn, whatever she was doing here.

As he handed her the newspaper across the aisle…

"Yes, the Europass is a good idea. You can travel just about anywhere in Europe." Tupelos tried to sound pleasant.

"And where are you headed? Are you an American?"

"No…" Tupelos was not sure if he should say he was from Spain or even say where he was going. "No, I am not American. I'm sure you can tell by my accent."

"From Spain, I gather?"

"That's right." Feeling more and more closed in, Tupelos knew he had to end the chitchat quickly. "And you…where are you heading, you mentioned a conference, in Lyon?"

Tupelos never could have imagined in a million years the purpose of the venue.

"Yes…an Interpol conference: new standards for fingerprinting are the topic. Should be very interesting."

Juan Jose Garcia Tupelos knew immediately he was not continuing by train to Barcelona. *The trip will take me through Lyon. This bitch will be chattering the whole way!*

"You will have to excuse me." Tupelos gave no reason. He knew he had to get out of this conversation quickly at any excuse. He hoped his sudden departure would not be viewed suspiciously. *Who attends an Interpol conference on fingerprinting standards? Is she a cop? A fingerprint technician?*

The woman thought, *That was strange. Handsome guy but not very friendly. Well, let's see what is in the newspaper this morning.*

And so were the thoughts of Mary Innis, an American FBI agent traveling on a combination vacation and business trip.

Chapter 42
A Muted Reaction

"Herr Becker is very fortunate. The loss of blood could have been fatal. Quick attention to his wounds here at the hospital saved his life. It looks like he will make a full recovery." As the doctor checked Becker's I.V. drip, Claudette Becker listened. She stood next to the private room bed where Hans had been brought after surgery late Saturday night. It was now Sunday, the day after the attack.

"Thank you, Doctor…He seems unresponsive…Is he going to get better?"

Frau Becker spoke dispassionately despite the words of concern.

Mrs. Becker, forty-eight years of age, was still good looking. Her red hair was cut short and gave her a boyish appearance. Her face was slender with pencil-thin brown eyebrows, large brown eyes, a slim nose, a delicate chin, and still with a smooth and pink complexion—hints of her former life. Born and raised in Stuttgart, she was once a top fashion model in Munich circles. She and Hans had been estranged for several years. Hans, however, refused a divorce while Claudette would have welcomed a generous settlement although not the disgrace of having been "dumped" for another woman. She felt her beauty slipping day by day despite the exercise classes, expensive facials, and most recently, nutritional consultants.

The attending physician spoke to Mrs. Becker. "Frau Becker, it's the lingering effects of the anesthesia. Some patients recover less quickly. Your husband has had serious trauma done to his body. He still has a long way to go. Perhaps this afternoon, he will be more alert."

"I see. Well, I will check back then later with the nurses."

"Good day, Madame."

"Good day, Doctor."

As Mrs. Becker reached the hospital room door…

"Oh…Frau Becker…one more thing, you should know that Mr. Baxter and Mr. Daniels left an address and phone number where they can be reached should you wish to speak with them. They certainly saved your husband's life. I believe they are leaving the area tomorrow morning. Check with the nursing station for the number."

"Yes, thank you, of course."

As Mrs. Becker left the room, the surgeon frowned and shrugged his shoulders. *Didn't seem to appreciate that information now did she,* he thought to himself.

As it would turn out, Frau Becker never stopped at the nurse's station. She never called back that day either to check on Hans' condition. On Sunday evening, Hans, told of his wife's visit, only reacted with mild surprise that she had bothered to come at all.

Chapter 43
NYPD Heads to Barcelona

Detectives Joe MacLean and Hal Sweeney were off to Barcelona on Thursday morning, September 11. Detective Sarova of the Spanish National Police would meet them at Barcelona International Airport (BCN) and coordinate with NYPD the hunt for the alleged assailant of their citizen, Maria Angela Aquino.

By the 11th, Juan Jose Garcia Tupelos had been on the move. He decided to end his rail transport in Zurich. After hitching a ride to the outskirts of Zurich, Tupelos stole a motorcycle. The drive to Barcelona, if he made it that far without detection, would take almost ten hours. But in keeping with his previous outlook of one country at a time, first it was France, 160 miles southwest of the motorcycle heist.

In Tupelos' rush to exit Zurich, he missed the prominent third page story entitled, "Assassination Attempt on the Life of Porsche Executive," in Monday's German newspapers. The word "assassination" by the press triggered ugly memories with readers. Several political murders had occurred in Germany shortly after reunification. It was needless sensationalism from the normally reserved press. More importantly, Tupelos could not have missed the article had he seen the newspapers and thus discovered that Hans Becker had survived the "assassination attempt."

The newspaper article continued saying that doctors at the Robert Bosch Hospital in Stuttgart said Becker would survive.

"Wanted for questioning is Jose Garcia Tupelos." The newspaper had gotten the name wrong. The newspaper said two Americans on holiday and business associates of Hans Becker had provided a description of the attacker to the police. The two witnessed the assault. In was the Americans' tentative identification, said the press, that led police to a Stuttgart hotel where the assailant was staying. Fingerprints in the hotel room matched prints found on the knife left at the scene of the assault by the perpetrator.

"Garcia Tupelos is probably armed and very dangerous," concluded the article.

Tupelos' photo was prominent to the right of the article. Robbery as a possible motive was buried amid the sensationalism.

Juan Jose Garcia Tupelos did reach Barcelona on his motorcycle by Wednesday, September 10. He had gotten across the border between France and Spain by taking several back roads he had once explored a few years before during his earlier days as a biker.

The police were now on his trail. Mary Innis, the woman who had a brief conversation with Tupelos on the train from Stuttgart to Zurich, saw the newspaper article and photo.

She called the police.

Innis placed Tupelos on the *Cisalpino* on Sunday morning after the attack.

"He got off at Zurich."

In addition, unlike the photo of Tupelos in the newspaper, she added, "He has no hair!"

The German police thanked her for her cooperation. After all, she was FBI!

Chapter 44
Reviewing the Facts

Thursday September 11, Barcelona, Spain

Joe and Hall disembarked the Boeing 747 United Airlines flight, breathing a sigh of relief when the jet landed safely. Joe and Hal as well as many of the passengers had expressed concern on this anniversary of the horrific terrorist attack.

The day was gloomy as rain pounded the tarmac. Hal refused any sense of defeat, determined to look on the bright side of this, his first visit to Europe.

Hal trailed a few feet behind Joe as they disembarked. In an attempt to project his voice towards Joe, Hal said forcefully...

"Joe, how are we going to recognize Sarova?"

Joe turned slightly back saying, "Don't worry, the chief said Sarova will know us when we arrive. Probably meet us at the luggage claim."

"The rain...in Spain...falls...main...lee on the play... ain," the song came from Hal's lips.

"I don't believe it." Joe slowed down as Hal pulled abreast.

"Call it osmosis...or maybe we have worked too long together...something." Hal's large smile filled his Irish face.

The escalator took Joe and Blimp down to the luggage area.

"We might be singing another tune down here, Blimp. Let's hope all our stuff arrived ok."

"Detective MacLean? Detective Sweeney? How do you do?"

Rodrigo Vicario Sarova was a small man of sixty years at 160 pounds and about five feet eight inches. He was slim and impeccably dressed in a designer gray suit with paisley tie. The disparity to Joe and Hal's casual look was plain for all to see. Sarova's thinning black hair was stylishly groomed. His dark eyes and small mouth seemed in contrast as a powerful hawk is to a songbird.

He was slight of build but with a firm handshake, as Joe and Hal next realized.

"Yes, but how did you know?" said Joe extending for the handshake.

"Call it instinct? Or maybe because the other two guys coming off the plane together were holding hands?" Sarova smiled and shook Hal's hand with equal firmness.

"Oh that's good, very good. No we work together but we don't live together," said Joe with a chuckle in his voice.

"Since it is almost dinner time, at least by your American standards, I have arranged for my driver to take us to a local restaurant and then I will accompany you to your hotel where the business part of the evening will take place."

Hal looked at his wristwatch, realizing he had forgotten to turn it ahead by six hours.

"The local time is 6:45 p.m.," commented Sarova as he saw Blimp looking around the terminal for a clock.

"This way, Detectives." Sarova directed the NYPD representatives to a terminal exit and his waiting white police van brightly labeled with the insignia for the Spanish State Police, a dark blue shield with one broad yellow ban bordered by two narrow red bans setting off the words *Cuerpo Nacional De*...from...*Policia.*

Ernesto, Sarova's youthful bodyguard also with the National Police, joined the three men. The young officer wore the National Police blue-with-gray-trim uniform. He had first gone to gather the visitors' luggage.

As they settled into the police van, Joe and Hal took the back seat with Sarova and his bodyguard/driver upfront.

"Actually, Detectives, your Chief Brennan faxed this over last night."

Sarova turned to the detectives in the back seat and held up the fax photos of Joe and Blimp as both leaned slightly forward to get a better view.

"Oh god, those are awful photos," said Blimp holding back his usual insult of the chief.

The three had a good laugh, and later, a good dinner. By 9:30, the three detectives gathered in Joe's room at the Melia Barcelona Hotel in downtown Barcelona.

"Before we get down to business, gentlemen, I want you to know I will meet you in the hotel restaurant for breakfast. We will show you a few sights afterwards and then it will be off to Gran Canaria. How does that sound?"

Joe and Hal agreed.

"Now here is what we know, Detectives."

Sarova pulled back the cherry wood chair that accompanied the hotel room's writing desk, turning the chair to face Joe who was moving to the large sofa. Hal sat on the bed. He caught himself instinctively beginning to look for his notepad.

Joe made himself comfortable as he kicked off his shoes and relaxed on the sofa. He placed his right leg up on the cushions. The left leg dangled a few inches off the carpeted floor. He curled his toes releasing the fatigue of the day.

Sarova spoke to both detectives, "I am sure you realize we have no motive beyond robbery. Obviously, it seems a long way to go just to rob someone. So I know you have ruled out a simple robbery."

Joe answered, "Absolutely. You read in the file we sent, the woman had no identification. It became obvious through the investigation that the killer didn't want us to know who she was."

Despite the seriousness of these words, Joe relaxed more deeply as he raised the left leg to the sofa and, finding a comfortable pillow, rested his head.

"And so, Detectives," replied Sarova as he maintained a rigid posture in the wooden chair, "if we are dealing with a hired killer, then we must have someone who hired him?"

Hal now spoke up still sitting on the edge of the bed reluctant to stretch out knowing this was Joe's room.

"And did you find out anything about this Aquino woman, Rodrigo?"

"We have found out that her and her sister, and apparently also a brother-in-law, operate a health spa on the Canaries. We have not yet told them of the woman's death since we believe one or even both of them could be suspects. In fact, I have ordered a surveillance of the relatives to see what that may turn up."

"What could be behind that scenario?" said Joe.

Rodrigo Vicario Sarova gave no answer.

"And the last item for tonight! A Mary Innis of the United States, an FBI agent on part holiday in Europe but on her way to Lyon for an Interpol workshop, positively identified Tupelos as a passenger on an express train from Stuttgart to Zurich."

"Stuttgart, Germany." Hal sounded proud of his knowledge of world cities.

"Yes, evidently," continued Sarova with a combined tone of regret yet urgency, "Tupelos robbed and left for dead a German auto executive near the executive's hotel. I have spoken to Helmut Bassen of the State Police of Baden-Wurttemberg. Tupelos is the prime suspect. They have witnesses and fingerprints. An all-points alert led to the agent's identification of Garcia Tupelos. She did mention that, unlike his photo, he has shaved his head."

Sarova took a deep breath and continued...

"We are now looking for a connection, if there is any, between the Aquino murder and the apparent attempted murder of the executive."

"It seems an odd pair of victims, a Canarian health spa owner murdered in the Bronx and an auto executive assaulted in Germany," replied Joe still resting comfortably on the sofa.

"Indeed. Well, we also believe Garcia Tupelos is already in Spain. Perhaps right under our noses here in Barcelona. We know he fled Switzerland on a stolen motorcycle. He still could be in France, of course."

Hal could not resist any longer. He made himself comfortable on Joe's hotel room bed. Joe looked over but did not object. Then Hal had a thought.

"You know the connection...the connection between the health spa and the auto executive? Maybe the guy was once, or perhaps often, a customer of the spa. I read that lots of Europeans vacation down there, isn't that right, Rodrigo?"

"Yes, that's right. Well, that is something we are looking into. As of now, I don't believe the auto executive is in a condition to speak to the police."

Then, after seeing the fatigue manifested in both the American detectives, Sarova commented, "I think you both need some rest."

Sarova pushed the chair back under the desk and started to move for the door. Joe stood and began walking in his stocking feet to see Sarova out. Hal continued to lie on the bed.

"Thank you for dinner, Rodrigo. It was wonderful." Joe patted his very full stomach.

"I will call on you here at 8:30 for breakfast?"

"We will meet you in the hotel restaurant at 8:30," replied Joe as the two men stood at the hotel room door.

"Well, goodnight then." Sarova raised his right hand and waved to Hal. Hal lifted his right hand and gave an exaggerated hand wave to Sarova.

Little did the three realize, but Hal had stumbled exactly on the connection between Hans Becker of Stuttgart,

Germany, and Maria Angela Aquino of Gran Canaria, Spain.

Chapter 45
Spanish Hospitality

"Is that where we get the word gaudy from?" inquired Joe.

"To tell the truth, I am not sure," said Sarova.

Detective Vicario Sarova was pointing out several of the spectacular designs throughout Barcelona that were the work of the Spanish architect Antonio Gauda, or Gaudi in the English spelling.

As the bodyguard/driver meandered through the avenues of Barcelona, Detective Sarova proudly pointed out some of the history of the city. Gaudi designed buildings such as the

Casa Mila, or apartment house, with its curvy stone façade and cast-iron balconies in the form of masks, a combination of the Gothic and Moorish styles. In another part of the city, Joe and Hal viewed the site of the 1992 Summer Olympics with its history-making opening spectacular. The American detectives admired the harbor area with its container ships and cruise ships anchored in the placid and splendidly cobalt blue Mediterranean waters.

Nothing, however, would be as impressive to Joe and Hal as the Church of the Holy Family or *La Sagrada Familia*, the symbol of Barcelona to the entire world.

"Every side of the church is different…truly amazing!" commented Joe as the police van circled the cathedral, taking in its entire architectural splendor.

Joe was commenting on not only the elaborate eighteen spires or towers symbolizing the twelve apostles, four evangelists, the Virgin, and Jesus Christ, but also the expressionist designs on each side of the church. The designs gave this twentieth-century cathedral four different entrances—four different interpretations of the mysteries of faith.

"The church is still under construction. It was begun in 1886, but today, with modern equipment, it will be finished in a year or two, provided the money keeps coming in from the faithful," emphasized Sarova.

All this, however, was a morning prelude to an early afternoon flight to Gran Canaria aboard the local carrier for the Canaries: Binter Airlines.

*****

Friday, September 12th had been enjoyable enough with the Barcelona sightseeing, the pleasant flight (more like an excursion thought Joe) to Gran Canaria, and the delicious home-cooked late-time dinner. Joe and Hal had enjoyed the festivities at the home of one of Rodrigo Vicario Sarova's relatives on his mother's (Vicario) side of the family. Their home was just off the Calle Triana de Mayor near the old city.

Saturday, however, was about to jolt Joe and Hal back to reality.

The hunt for Angela Aquino's murderer would lead to some surprising developments.

Chapter 46
The Investigation Widens

Joe and Hal settled into their spacious rooms at the Melia Confort Iberia Hotel located alongside Las Palmas' seaside promenade. Saturday, however, would not be a day of sightseeing or even much relaxation. Along with Detective Sarova, Joe and Hal would be checking out a number of leads including the last known residence of Juan Jose Garcia Tupelos. At least that was the plan.

Very contrary to Joe and Hal's comfort levels, Detective Sarova asked both detectives to surrender their weapons. Sarova motioned to his holster carrying an Astra A-75 Firefox semi-automatic.

"I am sorry, but you are my guests. We must lead the investigation."

Joe and Hal relinquished their Glock G18C fully automatic revolvers. About half of the NYPD used the Glock model.

Surrendering the pistols unsettled Joe. Joe would soon have every reason to worry.

Nevertheless, Joe and Hal eagerly wanted to continue. After all, they had come over 3,000 miles to "get their man."

"Perdon, Señora...Entiente usted Ingles?" Sarova took the investigative lead as the three detectives along with the driver/bodyguard began searching the old haunts of Tupelos hoping to turn up his whereabouts. Their first stop was his apartment in a not so good section of Las Palmas.

The property owner spoke some English indicating she had not seen Tupelos for "...about two weeks, and if he doesn't pay rent by the end of the week, I will have...him evicted."

"No," said the landlady she did not know where he went. Perhaps, she had added, the woman at the health shop in the old city would know. She indicated that she knew Tupelos "hung out" there.

Because the Spanish police had ordered surveillance on the comings and goings of Patricia and Erik Ruegar, Sarova surmised that the property owner was referring to the Be at Your Best Health Foods Store. The police had noticed that Erik Ruegar frequented the store. Perhaps that was a possible link to Tupelos. A talk with the health food storeowner could move the investigation forward.

Confirming the comings and goings of Erik Ruegar was the first goal for Sarova.

At the health food store, Bridget Olsen said she knew Erik Ruegar.

Sarova placed a photograph on the counter.

"Do you know this man? He goes by the name of Juan Jose Garcia Tupelos."

"I don't know anyone by that name. I don't know this man."

Bridget Olsen pushed back the photo of Tupelos toward Detective Sarova.

On entering the shop, Sarova had introduced himself but deliberately left out any introductions of the NYPD.

Upon Sarova's insistence, Bridget Olsen looked again at the photo of Tupelos. In response to Sarova, she said that if he did come into the store, she didn't remember.

"Well, Miss, you do know an Erik Ruegar?" Joe believed the busty blonde wearing a revealing pink V-neck and tight jeans was telling the truth about not knowing Tupelos. Since she did not know about the surveillance of Ruegar, Joe felt the question would test her honesty if she were pressed for more information about Ruegar.

"I told you I know Erik Ruegar. What's this all about?"

Bridget Olsen became visibly nervous. She was also surprised that the detective questioning her seemed to be an American.

"Is something wrong? Is Erik alright?"

"Should there be something wrong, Miss?" interjected Detective Sweeney combining his question with a mischievous Leprechaun smile.

Olsen thought, *Two American detectives?* Then hesitantly, she added...

"Look, Erik and I are friends. Did his wife send you here?"

Rodrigo, Joe, and Hal all glanced at one another, all thinking the same thing, *Let the fools speak!*

"And why, Miss Olsen, would three detectives... excuse me, Miss Olsen, I should have properly introduced Detectives MacLean and Sweeney of the New York City Police Department. Why would Mr. Ruegar's wife have sent us?"

"Well, you know...perhaps she thinks Erik and I are having an affair...jealousy, you know. But why are American police involved?"

Sarova ignored the question and continued, "Miss Olsen, what exactly is your relationship with Mr. Ruegar?" Sarova sensed it was more than sex.

"Ok...Erik does come here often to see me. He does buy stuff and such here. Vitamin supplements and..." Bridget paused and thought that the police were investigating illegal steroids. "Not here, I know nothing about steroids. Maybe down the street at the gym they will know about that."

"That's it?" Joe knew there had to be more.

Bridget Olsen's thoughts were racing. She did not know what to make of all these questions. "Erik has also borrowed money from me. He said he needed it for a business deal."

"How much money? What kind of a deal?" It was Sarova's turn to be skeptical.

"I gave him 5,000 Euros. All he told me was that he wanted to start his own business. I never questioned him any further."

Hal now asked the question. "And when was this, this loan of the money?"

"I think it must have been about three to four weeks ago."

Hal continued, "Did he say what kind of business?"

"No, he just said that he had to make a down payment on a business."

Detective Sarova felt at this point that they were not going to get any more useful information out of Bridget Olsen. The fitness center was next on the agenda.

Sarova reflected, *What was that about steroids?* Sarova was not even sure about the laws in Spain regarding steroids. *I have been in homicide for ten years! What do I know about steroids?*

The fitness center was only a few yards up along the promenade. As they walked slowly, the three detectives began to reflect on what Olsen had said and on what she had not said.

Hal spoke first. "You think, Joe, you'll loan me $5,000? I am not going to tell you for what. Just give me the dough."

"Right away, old buddy."

"I have to say, Detectives, that she struck me as the kind of woman who might just give the guy money. She owns a store, appears to be doing well, yet she didn't appear to be too intelligent. Thoughts all over the place."

Sarova was tacitly agreeing with Hal—you have to be dumb to give money out and ask no questions.

Joe smelled something else.

"She seemed eager to tell us about the loan, but she was nervous thinking about Mrs. Ruegar's involvement. Maybe Ruegar spoke in not so glowing terms about his wife, and, come to think, why would Ruegar go to this woman for money. It seems that he didn't want his wife to know about the so-called business arrangement."

Hal believed there was more in what was not said.

"Joe...Rodrigo...I think there's a good chance that Ruegar needed the money as a payment to Garcia Tupelos. We know Tupelos killed the sister-in-law in the Bronx. We are trying to find out why. Perhaps this Ruegar is behind the murder."

Hal again displayed thoughtful insight.

"Then we have to find out if the assault on the auto executive in Germany has any connection to this. If it does, there would appear to be a larger motive. I am going to find out," answered Sarova.

Rodrigo Sarova motioned to his bodyguard who was trailing a few yards behind to catch up and walk astride with them along the promenade.

"Ernesto!" Sarova instructed his man to get back to the police van and call immediately to find out all that the German police knew about Hans Becker and whether he had ever been to Gran Canaria and if he knew Olsen or the Ruegars.

The Canarian sun shone brightly on the promenade; no graffiti here, no trash or refuse, no decay. The promenade was busy with shoppers and late summer tourists.

The three men came upon the Las Palmas Fitness Center. The yellow sign with black lettering mirrored the sun. A stick figure lifting a barbell emblazed the front door entrance. Through the two large windows on each side of the door was fitness equipment ready to test the endurance of customers.

Detective Sarova again started the questioning.

Miguel Vargas, the manager, was showing a female how to use one of the machines when the three men entered. The smell of perspiration brought Joe's fingers to his nose in a futile attempt to block the stink. It did not seem to affect

Rodrigo and Hal. Joe had to remember: *I just don't like the odor; it reminds me of the zoo.*

Joe ignored reality since he was a user of health clubs himself.

"*Perdon, señora*, I am with the Spanish State Police. We have some questions for the owner."

Miguel indicated to the female on the treadmill that he would be only a moment.

"I am the owner-manager. My name is Miguel Vargas. Is there a problem?"

Detective Sarova again did not introduce the NYPD detectives. Miguel looked quizzically at the two men accompanying the State Police officer but said nothing. Then for some inexplicable reason, reflected Joe and Blimp, Sarova chose to ask about Erik Ruegar and not Tupelos.

Joe and Hal appeared stunned. Did Sarova know something he was not telling them? How did this become an

investigation about Ruegar? Tupelos was the first priority…
or was he?

Joe thought, *First he takes our weapons, now he takes
our suspect?*

"Does Erik Ruegar use this facility and has he been in
lately?"

"Yes, he was in yesterday afternoon. Comes in
regularly."

With a wave of the hand, Sarova stopped Joe from
asking any questions as he politely and silently signaled
Joe and Hal to let him alone do the questioning. Joe and
Hal remembered the chief's order, "I want NYPD to get this
guy!" *What was Sarova trying to pull here?*

"Anything unusual in Mr. Ruegar's behavior over the
last two or three weeks?"

Miguel did not have to think long for an answer. He
hated Erik Ruegar and his condescending attitude. *Mickey,
Mickey, fuck you, Mickey, just do it!*

"Yes, if you wait a moment, I need to go to my desk."

Detective Sarova's eyes followed Vargas to the desk behind the reception counter. Joe looked absently about. Hal glanced at the attractive female on the treadmill.

In a few moments, Miguel returned. He held some scraps of paper.

"Erik has been asking me to take messages for him, like I'm some kind answering service. I put up with it, but I don't like it. I made a copy of the numbers for my records. I don't allow customers making long distance calls from the office. I thought Erik might try that. He didn't. But, anyway, here...here are two phone numbers that an unknown caller told me to give to Erik and not to call the spa. He and his wife own a place about thirty kilometers from here..."

"Yes, we know about that, continue please..."

"That's it...just these phone numbers. Except that here with this number..."

Miguel showed Rodrigo: 1-201-941-5145. "With this number, the caller said something strange…he was a male for sure…he said, 'One is an I.'"

"Eye the seeing thing or the personal pronoun?" Hal refused to be silent adding mentally, *You little gym bastard, stop wasting our time!*

Rodrigo gave up trying to keep NYPD out of the questioning.

"What do you make of it, Joe?"

"Except for that eye or 'I' business, it's a New Jersey phone number. I know, my wife has a sister out there and I see the phone charges out to Jersey."

Miguel glowed. Ruegar was in trouble.

"There's more. When I gave him that number, he was unusually pleased. He generally has a sour disposition. That day, Bridget wasn't here either, I don't think. He's especially annoyed when he can't feast his eyes on her."

"You mean Bridget Olsen, from the health foods store?" Joe's mind was stringing the information together quicker than an old computer with 32K: *Bridget Olsen, Erik Ruegar, Patricia Ruegar, and Juan Tupelos? Maybe this Becker person?*

"And the second number?" Hal inquired.

By now, Miguel had guessed correctly that the two other men were police from America. *That son-of-a-bitch Erik is in big trouble!*

"Right...here: 1-355-209-2930. That time, there was no special instructions."

"Recognize this one, Joe?"

"No way...that's an odd one...certainly not from the New York metropolitan area."

"No problem. As soon as Ernesto gets back, he will check it out for us."

Simultaneously with this comment, Rodrigo looked to the front door hoping Ernesto would return and join them in the fitness center.

Sarova continued, "Can you give us an approximate date and time that these calls came in, these two numbers, that is?"

"Oh, it was three times, Detective!"

"Three?"

"The first time it was that 201 number. The second time that 355 number. And the third time it was the 201 number again with the same 'One is an I' business."

"And what about when?"

"I remember the second 355 number because Mr. Ruegar was very rude. It was on the first, September 1. I almost had a fight on my hands between him and George. George was a guy who signed up that day for the club. Ruegar, like I said, was happy to hear the 201 number, maybe that was about a week or ten days before. But with this number, he had a very puzzled look on his face. Like maybe it wasn't good news, I thought."

Hal was frustrated with the health club manager's answers. Usually sharp as a tack, Hal was not following this one. He quickly added...

"What about the third call? The second time for the 201 number, that is. When did you tell Mr. Ruegar about that call?"

"Yes, I remember it well. It was last Saturday night. I was closing up the club. Must have been about 9:15 or so. The same message 1-201-941-5145. But I never told Erik. I said to the caller, 'Yeah, one is an I, right?' and slammed the phone down. I was fed up with the whole scene. I never told Ruegar."

The entire discussion, thought Joe, circled on Ruegar! Whatever happened to the Tupelos investigation? Joe had to ask. He was getting annoyed with Sarova's line of questioning. *Interesting, but what the hell did all the phone numbers prove?*

Without Sarova's permission, if that was what he needed at all, Joe took out a photo from a brown manila folder. Joe showed the health club manager a photo of Tupelos.

As Vargas was looking at the photo, Rodrigo Sarova looked toward the back and to the right of the fitness center where the shower rooms refreshed the clients.

Sarova cringed. His right hand went suddenly to his holster.

Joe asked, "Mr. Vargas, has this man ever been in this club?"

"Why, sure. There he is right over there!"

Chapter 47
Establishing a Link

Hans Becker was recovering nicely. Additional surgery was required to repair the left leg since the priority that night in the Robert Bosch Hospital emergency room was the stab wound in Becker's side that had scarred the kidney. A week later, Saturday the 13th, the same day Sarova and the American detectives were searching for Tupelos, Becker was on the mend. The doctors had said perhaps another five to seven days in the hospital.

Becker had many visitors, mostly associates from the auto industry. Several had inquired about the attack, asking

Hans if the newspaper's version of the attack might be true, that it was an assassination attempt.

"I never saw the man in my life. As far as I am concerned, this was a simple robbery attempt." Becker felt comfortable in the explanation.

Becker had related this conclusion to several executive friends from Porsche, BMW, and Daimler-Chrysler.

"Not to worry, gentlemen, I don't think our rivals are trying to bump off the best and brightest of German auto; after all, that would leave **me** out!"

But among the visitors who did not come to see Hans, except for that first day when he was still drowsy from the anesthesia, was Frau Becker. She had sent a nice card and a bouquet of flowers, but that was it. Hans could only think…*Hell has no fury like a woman scorned!*

On Saturday, Hans would have a visitor. Helmut Bassen of the German State Police apologized for the intrusion but related that the Spanish police as well as two New York City homicide detectives were on the trail of his alleged assailant. They needed information immediately. Translations....

"Have you ever been on holiday or perhaps business in Las Palmas or any one of the islands Canaries?"

"Yes, several times."

"Do you know a Bridget Olsen?"

"Who?"

"Do you know Erik Ruegar?"

"Yes, I do, why?"

"Do you know Angela Aquino?"

"Yes, she owns a health spa with her sister down there. I along with several executives have enjoyed the facilities. We are good friends."

Bassen excused himself saying that he had to make a phone call but would return to the hospital room shortly.

The questions puzzled Hans. He drew no inferences from the New York City Police tracking down his assailant and the fact that Angela had taken a business/pleasure trip to the United States.

Bassen phoned the Spanish State Police to relay the call to Ernesto who was waiting in the police van to inform Sarova of what he had found out.

"You can tell Sarova that there is a definite link between Aquino, the Ruegars, and Hans Becker," related Bassen.

This was the information Sarova back in Las Palmas was waiting for.

Ernesto knew it was urgent. He had parked the police van one long block from the health foods store where he last knew Sarova to be. He walked quickly, then, sensing a particular urgency, began to run. The cobblestones under his feet caused the powerfully built police officer to flinch with the thumping on the less-than-smooth surface.

"They left about fifteen minutes ago. I think they went over to the fitness club down the promenade, that way."

Bridget Olsen, seeing enough police for the day, took Ernesto's arm and walked him briskly to the front door of her store. She pointed to the club some thirty yards away.

Ernesto trotted toward the health club with more than a few bystanders and shoppers turning in alarm at a uniformed police officer dashing thorough the ordinarily peaceful Vegueta.

The tranquility of the promenade would quickly be shattered.

Chapter 48
A Sudden Turn of Events

Saturday turned out to be a slow day at the Spa at San Agustin. Erik, not having heard from Tupelos, became concerned that something had gone wrong. He decided to forego his responsibilities at the spa and motor his Nighthawk on the thirty-mile trip up to Las Palmas. A face-to-face talk with Miguel was the plan. For the past few days, Erik had not asked about any calls for him. He was noticing Miguel's anger over the messenger service routine and figured he had better back off for the time being. Nevertheless, he thought, *I should have heard from Tupelos by now.*

It was 11:10 a.m. when Erik parked his Nighthawk and walked over to the fitness facility. He strolled on the promenade, about twenty yards from the center....

*****

At the same moment...

Ernesto was hurrying to the fitness center, shoppers and pedestrians alarmed by his quick pace in this normally placid promenade of shops, cafes, and two- or three-storied apartments with wrought-iron balconies overlooking the comings and goings...

*****

At the same moment...

Sarova cringed. His right hand went suddenly to his holster.

"Mr. Vargas, has this man ever been in this club?"

"Why, sure. There he is right over there!"

The three detectives turned in unison toward the front door. Sarova had already drawn his weapon. He had recognized Garcia Tupelos as the wanted man emerged from the locker room to the detectives' right as they were questioning Miguel Vargas.

Despite their years of experience, the sudden turn of events startled Joe and Hal. Thinking froze as they spotted Tupelos running to the front door.

Tupelos knew immediately what was happening. *Three cops no doubt! They have turned in my direction. The small guy has a weapon. Got to get the hell out of here fast!*

The burly Ernesto appeared at the front door of the fitness center.

"Ernesto, stop him, that man with the blue tee!" Sarova was rushing to the front door in an attempt to stop Tupelos.

Tupelos charged and bolted over the larger framed Ernesto, knocking him to the ground. Ernesto straddled the doorway, the police officer's legs in the gym, his torso sprawled on the promenade.

Ernesto reached for his revolver, tugging furiously, trying to get a grip on the revolver from his prone position.

Tupelos was on all fours as he scrambled past Ernesto. He stood and drew a revolver from a small satchel. He reached the promenade just a few feet outside the door. Still standing wobbly from the impact of the collision with Ernesto, Tupelos stumbled backward trying to put distance between himself and the prone officer.

The quiet of the promenade was no more.

Tupelos saw Ernesto reaching for his weapon. Tupelos fired, getting two wild shots off as bystanders and shopkeepers enjoying the midday sun screamed, scurried about, shouted… "Shots, shots, he's shooting over there!"

Ernesto screamed in pain as a bullet pierced his right shoulder. Another bullet ricocheted off the red-orange cobblestones of the promenade. Tupelos furiously tossed his satchel, flinging it towards the wounded officer as if it could do more damage.

Sarova emerged from the fitness center. He stooped over his wounded comrade. Joe and Hal reached the injured officer.

Joe thought...*No fucking weapons and here we are in the middle of a gun battle.*

Sarova went to his knees tending to the wounded Ernesto.

Tupelos ran, now some ten yards away and heading for what he hoped would be his escape route, the busy vehicular roadway another twenty yards distant.

MacLean picked up Ernesto's Astra A-75. Sarova did not notice.

The Astra revolver felt clumsy, heavier than his usual Glock.

MacLean ran several yards in pursuit of the fleeing fugitive.

The pedestrians had scattered, some were lying face down on the promenade. Several women in balconies above pointed in the direction of Tupelos' escape route. Shopkeepers had arrived cautiously to their stores'/cafés' front doors, looking aghast or crouching to a squat to avoid any bullets.

Joe MacLean stopped. He lifted the Astra revolver. He aimed. It was a clear shot!

Juan Jose Garcia Tupelos fell mortally wounded to the promenade.

Within seconds, Joe reached the dying Tupelos. Sarova arrived a few seconds behind. For the moment, Hal watched over Ernesto. Sarova knelt next to Tupelos. Joe stood surveying the scene. A crowd slowly began to gather around the gunman, his blood muddled with the cobblestones below his almost lifeless body.

"Give me the gun, Joe." Sarova suspected a pile of trouble with an American detective shooting a suspect on his watch.

It happened again. Joe lost concentration on the matters at hand, *A promenade...a promenade for death...a rude promenade.*

"MacLean, give me the goddamn gun," shouted Sarova.

Joe handed Sarova the weapon. Sarova quickly placed the gun in his jacket pocket.

"How's Ernesto?" Joe was back in the present tense.

"Hal is calling for an ambulance and more backup. He's been hit in the shoulder. I think he'll be ok."

Concern for his comrade masked for the moment his annoyance with Joe MacLean.

*****

Almost at the same moment...

Erik heard the commotion on the promenade. *What the hell is going on?* He picked up his pace wanting to be part of the action.

As Erik was one of the first to reach the dying Tupelos, curiosity instantly became horror, panic, and a desire to flee. *Holy shit, I can't let him see me here!*

The crowd of onlookers had swelled to fifteen, maybe twenty. Erik began to move to the back of the crowd, squeezing in, out, and in between the onlookers.

As Erik reached the periphery of the crowd, Bridget ran up to Ruegar and clutched him around the waist.

"Oh my god, I saw the whole thing from the shop. I wonder if that's the guy the police were asking about just a few minutes ago in my store?"

Erik did not rehearse this response. "Really, the police were in your store? What did they want to know?"

"If the guy ever came into the store? I said no. I thought maybe they were asking about steroids with all the questions these days."

"What did you tell them, Bridget?"

Ruegar's flight instinct was close to a sparrow trying to escape a tomcat.

"I...I...I...didn't say anything, Erik. I swear to God...I sent them away to...to...the gym."

Joe was looking back, standing slightly on his toes, trying to see if Hal was on his way to join him and Rodrigo. As he did so, he noticed the animated discussion between Bridget, whom he recognized from the interview, and the stranger.

Joe was quick...*That is Erik Ruegar, I will bet my life on it!*

"Look, Bridget, I'm going to have to leave you...got some...some business to look into. See you later."

Erik grabbed the blonde's delicate hands and arms, removing them from their grip around his waist. Bridget said nothing. She did not notice Detective Joe MacLean standing on his tiptoes and eyeing the pair above the crowd.

Joe squatted next to Sarova who was on the cell phone with emergency, requesting an ambulance for the wounded gunman.

"Listen Rodrigo, I think I saw Ruegar among the spectators. He seems in a big hurry. I'm going to follow him. He may lead us to something...someplace...or someone, helping to make sense of all of this."

"Ok, Detective Sweeney, I will return to the fitness place as soon as the ambulance arrives. We'll ask the manager a few more questions. Here, here is my number to the police van."

Joe followed about fifteen yards behind Ruegar. Ruegar was making his way to the parking lot and his Nighthawk. Joe surmised rapidly that he was going to need transportation. He eyed a young man heading to a motorcycle not too far from where Erik was approaching his motorcycle. *Whew...haven't driven one of these since my early motorcycle division days.* He stopped the young man and showed him his police badge—NYC police badge, that is.

"Listen, you have to let me drive your motorcycle. I know it's strange but this is police business. I have to follow that guy over there."

Joe heard and then saw the Nighthawk light up with power. "It's a matter of great importance, maybe life and death!"

"Not a chance, fella. You have no authorization," said the young man as he donned his helmet. Then to Joe's surprise...

"Climb aboard, we'll follow him together."

Joe figured hitching a ride on the motorcycle was better than any delay or a missed chance. He climbed aboard feeling slightly uncomfortably as he held on tightly to the motorcyclist's waist.

Garcia Tupelos could only mumble a few incoherent words before he died, the bullet having penetrated vital organs. The ambulance crew removed the body as Rodrigo and Hal returned to the fitness center where Ernesto was resting comfortably, attended to by another emergency team. Rodrigo told Hal on the way that Joe was following a man, Erik Ruegar he believed.

"Is he dead?" asked Miguel.

"Yes, he is, Mr. Vargas. We have a few more questions for you. Have you ever seen both Mr. Ruegar and the dead man together here in the club, talking...conversing, you know..."

"No, can't say I have, Officer. I'm here most of the time. Can't get any reliable help, so it's full time for me. I do know that Ruegar sometimes goes down to the nightlife area. It's about four streets from the Vegueto...that way." Vargas pointed to the rear of the health club.

Sarova continued with the questioning.

"I see. We will look into it. Mr. Vargas, why was Tupelos in here today? Did he work out often or what?"

"No, actually he just wanted to shower. Came in and left I think with the same clothes."

Mr. Vargas, could I see those phone numbers again?"

Sarova got on the police phone saying to his office. "Find out exactly where these numbers are located, Sergeant. I need the information right away."

Sarova had a strong hunch that the numbers might lead to where Joe was following Ruegar.

For the moment, Detective Sarova of the Spanish National Police and Detective Harold Sweeney, New York City Homicide Investigation Unit, headed for the bars and clubs of Las Palmas looking for motives.

"Just keep well behind, don't let him think we're following him." Joe's black and usually neatly combed hair was blowing in the breeze, his light summer jacket billowing from the air rushing past as the motorcycle reached the open road. It was the GC 1 leading from Las Palmas to Maspalomas and south.

Twenty-five miles…perhaps about twenty-five minutes later, Joe and his temporary deputy of sorts noticed Ruegar pulling into the parking lot of the four-star hotel, the Melia Tamarindos on San Agustin beach.

"Listen, thanks, thanks a lot. I will take it from here, I and Spanish Police, that is."

Joe shook the young motorcyclist's hand as he kept an eye on who he believed to be Erik Ruegar entering the lobby of the hotel.

"You're welcome. Definitely something to write home about!"

Joe followed Ruegar into the reception area. The atrium was spacious with eight wide steps clothed in red leading to the front desk and elevators. The highly polished brass rail supported Joe as he strode within just a few feet of Ruegar, trailing him to the elevators hoping the man would not recognize him as the second person on the motorcycle. He had no choice.

Joe entered the elevator with the man. Joe remained silent. The suspect pressed floor number 8. Joe pressed floor number 8. The man shifted on his feet several times, looking continually at the elevator's lighted indicators as the floors passed by…2…3…4…stop…The doors opened…an older woman got on the elevator. "Number 10, if you don't mind, young man."

The man had no reaction but obliged by pressing number 10. The elevator resumed its scaling of the building…5…6…7…8…stop. The man got out and turned left. Joe casually strutted out, turning right—supposedly. He looked back following the man down the blue-carpeted corridor. Fortunately, a bend in the hallway just ahead would hide Joe's inquisitiveness.

Joe turned the corner…stopped…turned and peeked around the corner and watched the suspect.

The man halted…knocked on one of the hotel room doors. He started to enter. Joe could only see an arm…it was an arm of a woman. Joe saw a bracelet dazzling bright from a graceful limb.

After waiting for a few minutes, Joe decided to check the room number where the suspect had entered. *I can check the hotel register and find out who is staying in this room.*

Joe gingerly walked down the hotel corridor. He stood in front of the door into which the man he believed to be Erik Ruegar had entered…room number 810. He pondered. *I'll wait down the hall to see if they come out together.*

Suddenly, the hotel room door unlocked and was opening, perhaps only a few inches. Joe dashed down the hallway looking for cover. He heard the man say loudly as he began to leave the hotel room….

"No…Patricia…no…I won't…I won't do it."

Joe heard no other voice as the man closed the door and headed for the elevator. The man entered the elevator.

Joe waited then darted into the stairway. *I'll get another elevator on the seventh floor.* As Joe entered the corridor of the seventh floor, he reached for the business card listing Rodrigo Sarova's phone number.

Joe planned to call Sarova when he reached the hotel lobby.

Chapter 49
In Search of a Motive

That same day back at Robert Bosch Hospital, Detective Helmut Bassen returned to Hans Becker's hospital room. Bassen had just finished placing the call to the Spanish State Police telling them of the connectivity among the Ruegars, Angela, and Becker.

Hans Becker recalled the German detective's recent questioning. He spoke in English.

"Well, Detective, why all these questions bout Miss Aquino und Ruegar, and who is Bridget anyway?"

"Herr Becker, what exactly is your relationship with Angela Aquino?"

"I told you we are friends. Is something wrong? Please tell me."

"Yes, I'm afraid so. Herr Becker…Angela Aquino is dead…"

Hans Becker, still hurting from his injuries, managed to lift his right hand to his face…Tears began to trickle down his ruddy cheeks. He was silent for the moment. He moved his right hand to his gray hair. Anguish then heartache were represented as the hand gripped the nape of his neck. His eyes closed tightly.

"It appears…Herr Becker…that she was murdered in the Bronx, New York, perhaps about three weeks ago. We believe the man who attacked you here in Stuttgart is also the man who murdered Miss Aquino."

"Oh god, Angela dead? Three weeks ago…did you say three weeks?"

"It appears that the assailant, a man named Juan Jose Garcia Tupelos, deliberately tried to hide the identity of his victim, for what reason we are still not sure. This is the reason why it took so long to identify the victim. The New York City Police are here in Europe, they are in Las Palmas now…they came to track down…this…Tupelos."

Bassen slowed his words. Becker was weeping. The sobbing causing him more pain coupled with his recovering wounds. Hans moaned out of pain and anguish.

"Herr Becker, do you what me to get the nurse?"

"No…no…I am just sad. It was more then friendship…I loved Angela."

As Becker lay in the hospital bed, his upper torso shook from sobbing. After a minute or two, Becker gathered himself enough and continued haltingly…"I have known… Angela…since she…since she vas a young woman. I tried to help the Aquinos after the father passed on. He worked for Porsche…I hired him you see."

"That leads me to another question, Herr Becker. Who would want to murder Miss Aquino?"

Becker looked up at the white ceiling of his private hospital room. His eyes were red. He looked ten years older from the stress of his injuries and the news that his paramour was dead. Hans looked out his sixth-floor hospital window, seeing the tops of tall buildings that made up the Stuttgart skyline beyond the campus setting that was Robert Bosch Hospital.

"Herr Becker? Do you know who would have wanted Miss Aquino dead…killed three thousand miles away no less?"

"Und me…this Tupelos want me dead, too? I thought it was a robbery?"

"It wasn't robbery. He left you for dead. The prints on the knife link him to a hotel in New York City. He was there a few days after the murder and then flew back to Spain."

"I don't know…I don't know who would want Angela dead. She was a very good promoter of the spa…maybe a competitor?"

"Not likely."

Becker's competitor question bought him time. His thoughts were racing…*Who?…Who?…Was Patricia that jealous?*

Or maybe the useless Erik…but to arrange this…not smart enough…or…

Becker did not dare fathom the thought.

Chapter 50
Cryptographers Bust the Code

Detectives Sarova and Sweeney saw Officer Ernesto Bolas taken to the local hospital for further treatment and convalescence. After they made their way back to the police van, Sarova called the station. Hal looked worried. *Joe?*

"Shouldn't we have heard from my partner by now? It's been more than an hour since he went on that one-man manhunt."

"Yes, I know. I'm worried, too. But I think what we may find out in a few moments will clear things up...maybe even tell us where your partner is right now."

Sarova spoke on the police phone.

"This is Detective Vicario Sarova. It's been about thirty minutes. We need to know about those telephone exchanges. It can't be that difficult. We know one is in New Jersey."

There was a short delay; static was coming through the police phone now on speaker so Hal could hear.

"Ah, yes, Detective. We called that 201 number. No one answered. We then asked the phone company out there to find out who the phone belonged to. They say it's a party named Jones; really, the name is Jones, but no record of them ever calling the number in Las Palmas."

"All right, so it was a bogus number then?"

"There's more, Detective Sarova. There is no such exchange as 355 anywhere in the world. Hard to believe, but true."

"Another bogus number?"

"Yes."

Rodrigo turned to Detective Sweeney who was feeling crowded and uncomfortable in the small police van contrasted to the big black Crown Victoria interceptor back in New York. Sweeney's legs were almost rubbing against the dash.

"What do you make of it, Detective?"

"Get your cryptographers on it. It is probably a code of some sort."

"Did you hear that, Sergeant? Run the numbers through our code-busting people. See what they can determine."

"Yes, Detective. Call you as soon as we have something."

Rodrigo and Hal decided to drive over to the bars and clubs. It was 1:45 p.m. The streets were empty with only a few early drinkers lifting the spirits of sorts. After about fifteen minutes and after checking out a few bars with no luck, they got a call on the police van phone from Joe MacLean.

"Joe, we were getting worried. Where are you?…What did you find out? Hal is with me here; we are checking the bars and clubs, trying to see if there is a connection between the murderer and the Ruegar fellow."

"Well, I'm at the front desk here of this plush hotel on San Agustin Beach, the Melia Tamarindos. The guy I followed, still can't say that he's Ruegar, but I can say for sure that he went to call on a woman here, a woman named Patricia…said something about not wanting to go through with something…overheard the conversation as he was leaving the room. What do you make of it?"

"I can't say. Did you check the registry?"

"Hold on, I'm doing that right now." Joe had convinced a skeptical hotel manager that his wanting to know the identity of the people occupying room 810 was truly "police business."

"Bingo, Rodrigo…Hal. The room is registered in the name of Mr. and Mrs. Ruegar. Seems like we have the contractors of our hired killer."

Hal spoke up. "It's all circumstantial, Joe. We have no proof of anything yet. Do you still have Ruegar in your sights?"

"No."

Sarova spoke. "Detective MacLean, let us plan to meet around 4:00 p.m. down in San Agustin, at the Ruegar spa. I'd say you're only about ten to fifteen minutes away. We have a few things here to check out yet; plus, we'll need a good forty-five minutes to get down there. I'll call for some backup to watch the place to see if the Ruegars show up. Don't try anything by yourself, Joe. You know we have the jurisdiction. I don't want you getting into any more hot water. While you're waiting, try your luck why don't you at the Casino Grand Canaria; it's in that hotel."

Joe thought, *Since when am I in hot water?*

"Ok...ok...but can you send a police car to give me a ride. One motorcycle ride for the day is enough."

Rodrigo and Hal looked at each other, and after a few seconds in unison, said, "Motorcycle ride?"

375

Sarova saw to it that a police car would give Detective MacLean a lift to the Spa at San Agustin at around 3:30.

It was 2:30 p.m. in Las Palmas where Rodrigo and Hal still needed to do more legwork. Joe, however, had an hour "to kill." He looked in his wallet. *140 American dollars; I think I'll stick to the quarter slots.*

Detectives Sarova and Sweeney tried still another club, a strip club called the Pony Express. American Western trappings decorated the club, including hobbyhorses of sorts for the strippers to undulate on and around.

Sarova handed the police photo of Garcia Tupelos to the bartender. He then presented his credentials. There were only a few drinkers in the place, no action on the stage. Yes, the bartender said that a man looking like the photo came in often. Sarova now attempted a link with Erik Ruegar.

"And how about a man named Erik Ruegar. Do you know that name?"

"Oh sure, he frequents the place."

"Did you ever see this Erik Ruegar and this man...this man in the photo...talking at some length?"

"I can't recall."

"All right then," interjected Hal, "was Ruegar ever in your club accompanied by a woman?"

"Yeah, on occasion, this woman came in with him, an older broad."

Rodrigo knew from checking out the Ruegar drivers' licenses that Patricia was older than Erik.

Just then, Sarova's police phone began to vibrate and ring, singing out to him that an urgent call was coming through. Sarova and Sweeney exited the strip club.

"Yes...this is Detective Vicario Sarova." The two detectives paused on the sidewalk next to their police van, standing under the red, white, and blue flashing "Pony Express" neon sign overhead. Then over the police phone...

"The code. It is a code detective. It was an easy code, too. Not much trouble figuring it out. You have your notepad? You have to write this down."

Hal pulled out his trusty notepad and motioned to Rodrigo that he would transcribe.

"Go ahead, what's the code?" said Rodrigo.

"Well, the 1-201-941-5145? The code people say it's the alphabet. Except for the first digit that is…ah…that appears to be an 'I' the letter, not the pronoun in English. Next 20 is 'T,' it's the twentieth letter of the alphabet…, then if you ignore the hyphens, here's the rest…"

Hal soon had it spelled out, in vertical form down his notepad:

I

20=**T**

19=**S** for the word **"it's."**

4=**D**

15=**O**

14=**N**

5=**E** for the word **"done."**

Hal rewrote the message, **"It's done."**

"And, Detective, the second number is a word, a date, and a time: 1-355-209-2930 the code people say it is '**Meet September 2, 9:30.**'"

Hal was quick again.

"Rodrigo, those codes were given to the fitness center owner to give to Ruegar. Remember the first and third times coincide with a murder, 'It's done,' meaning the job is done, the murder is done, except of course he failed to kill the auto executive, but he thought he did and so relayed that on to Ruegar."

"And, Hal, I think if we check out the Pony Express one more time and press the bartender a bit, we'll find out that Tupelos and Ruegar met on September 2, curiously a few days before the attack on Becker in Stuttgart."

The codes clearly implicated Erik Ruegar, implicated him largely because he had marginalized Miguel Vargas who ended up keeping the "phone numbers" and getting even. To arrest Erik Ruegar and his wife, Patricia Aquino Ruegar, was next. The charges would be murder and attempted murder.

It was not going to be that simple.

Chapter 51
The Bracelet Gleaming

"Damn it. I can never win at these slots."

Joe was moaning aloud as an elderly woman at a neighboring slot machine could only smile back at Joe's misfortune. Joe looked at his watch: *3:30...The car should be here any minute.*

"Detective MacLean?" The words were spoken by a uniformed woman police officer. "Detective, the hotel said you would be at the quarter slots...I'm Sergeant Carreira and I'm here to take you to join Detective Sarova."

"Yes, you came just in time. Lost bucks!"

An expression of contempt crossed the face of the elder slot machine player. *Police gambling while on duty. This is a disgrace.*

Joe handed the woman some leftover coins…contempt was exchanged with joy.

"We will be with Detective Sarova in a few minutes," commented the police officer as they entered the typical white-with-blue-decal police car of the *Cuerpo Nacional de Policia.*

The time was 3:50.

*****

Hal was mentally summarizing and reviewing his notes. The police van sped along the GC 1 on its way to the Spa at San Agustin. The time was 4:05. Rodrigo drove the police van with Ernesto in the hospital recovering from his wounds.

*****

"This is it, Officer Carreira? Nice place, I would say."

The police car was about to drop Joe MacLean off about thirty yards from the entrance to the Spa at San Agustin.

The time was 4:03.

"Perhaps, I wouldn't know; I don't frequent these places," replied the sergeant. "I will leave you off...It's...about 4:05...Detective Sarova will be here in a moment. I must return to my normal duties. Besides, we have a stakeout team here somewhere."

"Well, thank you for the lift, Sergeant. I think I will have a look around."

Out of habit, Joe leaned over from the passenger side of the police car ready to give the female sergeant a firm handshake. He stopped himself and instead gave Carreira a polite nod. He exited the police vehicle. Carreira drove off.

I will pretend I am a potential client, thought Joe as he walked the thirty yards and entered the facility. The stakeout team did not spot him.

The woman at the desk greeted Joe warmly. "Can I help you, sir? Here is a brochure that describes all of our services...sea mudpacks, algae baths, we have Thalosso Therapy, soap massage on a heated charka table..."

"Excuse me, what is Thalosso Therapy? Sounds very expensive."

"Not at all. Thalosso Therapy is simply a bathtub equipped with body jets for a gentle massage of the whole body. But we add to it essences of orchid, rose, or chamomile depending on your preference."

Joe turned and looked at the wall clock above the front entrance: 4:15.

Joe knew he needed to buy some time before Rodrigo and Hal arrived. He commented, "Thank you, I will let my wife decide. She will be along in a few minutes. I'll sit over there and look at the brochure."

"By all means. Make yourself comfortable. My name is Louise should you have any further questions."

As Joe began to turn toward the lounge area, another woman joined the woman at the reception desk. Joe heard...

"Ah, Patricia, I have given that gentleman a brochure. He is waiting for his wife."

Joe turned and smiled at the second woman now assuming the reception desk duties, *so that is Patricia Ruegar, our murderess? Our plotter? The reason I am 3,000 miles from New York?*

Joe took a long look at Patricia's left arm...the arm of the woman at the hotel? He had never attempted an identification based on a forearm, but there he was trying to match the picture in his mind of the left arm at the hotel with this left arm now clutching some papers on the reception desk counter.

It's not my jurisdiction...It's not my jurisdiction...Calm down, Joe...We'll all collar her together.

As Joe MacLean walked to the reception area pretending to show interest in the spa's brochure, the man Joe believed to be Erik Ruegar entered the spa through the front entrance. Joe hurried his walk to the lounge area and an easy chair, quickly masking his face with the brochure. *Holy shit, I hope he doesn't recognize me from the elevator.*

Joe looked at his watch. *4:18, where the hell are Rodrigo and Hal?*

Sarova's police radio announced…

"Detective Rodrigo Vicario Sarova, come in, please… Detective Rodrigo Vacario Sarova come in please…."

"Yes, yes, *si, si* this is Vicario Sarova, what is it?"

"Detective this is Sergeant Arroyo of the team assigned to the 'mudpack' stakeout."

Arroyo and another plainclothes officer were the officers assigned to the stakeout of the Spa at San Agustin, "Mudpack" being the code name.

Arroyo continued, "Quiet here, not much activity. A man on a motorcycle about two minutes ago. Just now, we see a woman exiting a cab. She is apparently making her way to the entrance. No other activity. All is quiet."

Hal peered over at Rodrigo who was looking for the turn off to the road that would take Hal and him to the spa. "The guy with the motorcycle must be Ruegar. It figures with Joe's comment about his own ride on a trailing motorcycle."

Rodrigo glanced at his watch. *Oh my, 4:10. We told MacLean 4:00.*

"Yes and the woman may be Mrs. Ruegar," added Rodrigo, "the timing is right, the woman at the hotel from the information we received from Joe."

Sarova saw the sign along the road advertising the "Spa at San Agustin."

Then, suddenly, from the mudpack stakeout detectives…

"Detective Sarova, are you…Detective…Arroyo here… come quickly…shots…We hear shooting." The police van's radio shouted danger.

Hal said, "What the hell?"

Rodrigo, "*Si…si…*a minute…will be there…will be there in a minute." *Oh, my god, I hope Joe did not take matters into his own hands! Again!*

Joe had not seen the shooter enter the spa.

BAM! BAM!…A pause then…BAM! BAM!…Bullets were flying in all directions.

Instinctively, Joe MacLean reached for his weapon. But he didn't have a weapon. The man he believed to be Ruegar was hit by the first two bullets and fell moaning to the tile floor about fifteen feet from Joe. The crimson blood of Erik Ruegar spilt on the orange-pink tile. The woman behind the front desk, Patricia Ruegar, Joe had surmised, ducked behind the reception desk as two more shots splintered the wood counter.

"Police, *polizia, polizia….Caiga su Arma!*" Joe shouted out in English and in the little Spanish he did know, enough to say, "Drop your gun."

With no weapon, Joe knew it was an idle threat.

As Joe yelled out, he saw that left arm…the delicate, fragile, graceful arm was now pointing the revolver at his head.

She was only twelve feet away.

Joe saw the wrist bracelet, the gold wristlet, the ring of tiny hearts around the left wrist, a delicate wrist it was…The bracelet glittered in the bright overhead lights of the reception area. *The bracelet, yes, I recognize it…the bracelet I saw in the hotel lobby.*

It's not my jurisdiction…It's not my jurisdiction…Shit, I'm a dead man.

A bullet whizzed by Joe's head as he dropped for cover.

Holy shit! Damn jurisdiction. No weapon! I must do something…

Then he heard, *"Polizia…Polizia…"*

BAM!

The woman tumbled to the cold tile floor clutching her shoulder. The revolver spun in circles across the floor.

Rodrigo Sarova stood in the doorway, his Astra revolver having discharged one very accurate but not deadly bullet. Detective Hal Sweeney brought up the rear with his loaded-from-Sarova Astra drawn in anticipation of more trouble.

Joe rushed over to check the condition of the wounded man. The man was in a bad state. Two bullets found their mark in his abdomen.

"Erik? Erik Ruegar? Is that your name?" Joe was on both knees talking slowly, deliberately, to the desperately wounded man.

"We'll call for an ambulance. Hang in there."

"Oh my god, oh my god, Erik, Erik, my Erik has been shot." The woman from behind the counter rushed to the side of the wounded man. She knelt down next to her dying husband.

Joe was confused, very confused. *Is this woman a murderess? Am I still in danger?*

And who the hell was the shooter?

*****

In his hospital bed...after Detective Bassen had left...

Hans Becker did not dare fathom the thought...but he knew.

The shooter was Claudette Becker.

Chapter 52
The Motives Revealed

It was July, two years before our story. The place was the home of Claudette and Hans Becker in Stuttgart, Germany; the situation, another argument between Claudette and Hans. Claudette was demanding a divorce.

Translation: "I am tired of your unfaithfulness, you, and that perky little bitch."

Claudette knew about Angela. Her circle of women friends knew about Angela. Claudette had become a joke.

Hans refused to consider divorce. His attitude was *So I have a paramour, a mistress. After all, Claudette is being less than honest about her own romantic interests.*

Translation: "Come on, Claudette. Your only need is to seduce a man younger than you. That's your need, isn't it; it always has been. 'I'm still the beautiful model of my twenties.'"

And so Claudette took a secret trip to the Canaries to meet with a former and still occasional lover. The place: The Pony Express, a few weeks before Erik Ruegar would meet Juan Jose Garcia Tupelos at the same club.

As Claudette Becker sat at the bar drinking her vodka martini, the bartender could not help but notice Erik Ruegar hitting on an older woman. *Christ, she must be twelve to fifteen years older, still not bad, though.*

Claudette spoke to Erik demanding change.

"All you are is a weed whacker, cutting bushes, or looking out for dirt bags hanging around the spa. I tell you, we can be free of both of them."

393

The bartender ambled down to the other end of the bar.

Frau Becker continued, "Find someone to do the job. I can put up $100,000. Hans is worth a million and with Angela out of the way...."

Claudette knew she could not overload Erik's psyche. Claudette never mentioned Patricia and "getting her out of the way." Frau Becker wanted Erik to have sole control of the spa for her own future and devious plans. After killing Angela and making Becker's death look like a robbery, Tupelos was to see to it that Patricia had an "accident."

*****

It was September at the Hotel Tamarindos, Room 810, on San Agustin beach.

Erik entered the room, agitated and nervous. "Tupelos is dead, the cops just shot him about forty-five minutes ago. I don't know if he killed Becker. What are we going to do now?

"Forget about Hans. I'll see to it he never leaves the hospital. Erik, you have to kill Patricia. It's the only way we will have everything...all the money we need. Make it an accident, with that car, have it go off the GC1 cliffs. You have to do it, Erik. Tupelos failed."

"Tupelos failed? When did Patricia become part of this?"

"I'm not going to be your mistress, Erik. This is the way it has to be if we are to continue."

"I will not kill my wife. No, I will not. This has to stop. Maybe they will not find the link between Tupelos, me, and you."

Erik spoke boldly. "Yes, **you,** Claudette...I'll tell them everything."

"Erik, you have to do it. There is no other way now. If not the accident, then here, take this pistol. You can make it look like robbery."

Erik Ruegar unlocked and opened the door a few inches to room 810.

Joe MacLean was just outside the door. He darted for cover.

"No...Patricia...No...I won't...I won't do it."

Erik Ruegar slammed the hotel door behind him. Claudette stood alone in the room. Then angrily and aloud, she said, "That cowardly bastard, just as I found out years ago...useless, good for nothing...good for nothing except sex."

Claudette Becker's rage would lead to the shooting death of her lover; a suicidal mission to be sure, going into the Spa at San Agustin and shooting Erik and attempting to kill Patricia. She did not plan on the Spanish National Police and the New York City Police thwarting her plan.

She confessed. Life in prison was the sentence.

Her good looks would not serve her well in prison.

Epilogue

It was three days after the shootings. Patricia Aquino Ruegar was still in shock, in total disbelief.

"You...Mrs. Ruegar, would have been the next victim of Claudette Becker's jealousy and rage," commented Rodrigo Sarova after the shooting, apprehension, arrest, and confession of Claudette Becker.

"Maybe because she thought she was going to die, or maybe because she wanted to clear her conscience, she admitted here in the spa that afternoon after she was shot, that she had a part in your sister's murder. Erik and Claudette planned to conceal the death of your sister long enough for you to have an 'accident.' She then planned to convince Erik to sell the spa and go away with her. Frankly, I think she probably wanted Erik eventually to meet with some kind of accident, too."

"And Hans? She wanted Hans dead?"

"She is saying that was more Erik's idea. She claimed that he was worried that Hans would figure out the intrigue. We will see what comes out in the trial, but in that assertion, she may only be looking for Hans Becker's sympathy. The prosecutor says Claudette Becker will be charged in your husband's death."

*****

Joe and Hal stayed in Las Palmas a few more days giving statements to the Spanish police. Joe had to explain the shooting of Tupelos. The detectives flew back to New York. The chief praised both detectives for "getting their man and their woman!"

Joe and Hal transferred to days. Liz and the kids were overjoyed.

Joe and Liz took a vacation in October to Savannah, Georgia—by plane! Joe especially loved Johnny Mercer memorabilia.

Hans completely recovered from his injuries. He retired to the Canary Islands. Patricia sold the Spa at San Agustin to the Melia Hotel chain. The hotel had the spa torn down, offering instead the sea mudpacks, algae baths, Thallaso Therapies, etcetera, at its own expanded and remodeled hotel spa.

The following summer, Hans and Patricia were married in a quiet ceremony.

After her body was brought back to the Canary Islands, Angela was laid to rest in the cemetery next to the Cathedral of Santa Ana, Vegueta—the old town, Las Palmas, Gran Canaria.

Patricia and Hans visited Angela's grave regularly, placing at the tomb a variety of colorful and fragrant flowers, most often,   Angela's   favorites—violets   and chrysanthemums.

The tombstone read:

THE WORLD WILL ALWAYS NEED DREAMERS. We love you, Angela.

About the Author

John Stephens is a former journalist, teacher, and school administrator now serving as an adjunct professor at a Pennsylvania university. He lives in Pennsylvania with his wife, Barbara Ann. This is his first work of fiction.

He grew up in Northern New Jersey. He attended Seton Hall University. Later, he earned advanced degrees at Pennsylvania State University and again at Seton Hall. After teaching private school in Connecticut and working there part-time as a newspaper reporter, John and his growing family moved back to New Jersey. He then served two public school districts as a teacher, supervisor, and school administrator.

"During all these years, I always wanted to write." With more time after retirement to enjoy travel and writing, Stephens began to research topics and write. In part, travel experiences in Europe are the basis of *Rude Promenade*.

When asked what influenced his desire to write, Stephens replied, "First, I taught American literature to high school students and loved it. Then I began to collect autographed books by American authors. Presently, I have approximately twenty-five signed novels." The list, said Stephens, includes, among others, William Faulkner, Jack London, William Styron, Willa Cather, and Robert Nathan. "I admire greatly these masters of the word and story. These are my heroes."

Printed in the United States
45250LVS00004B/1-69

9 781425 903268